SKYLANDERS SUPERCHARGERS

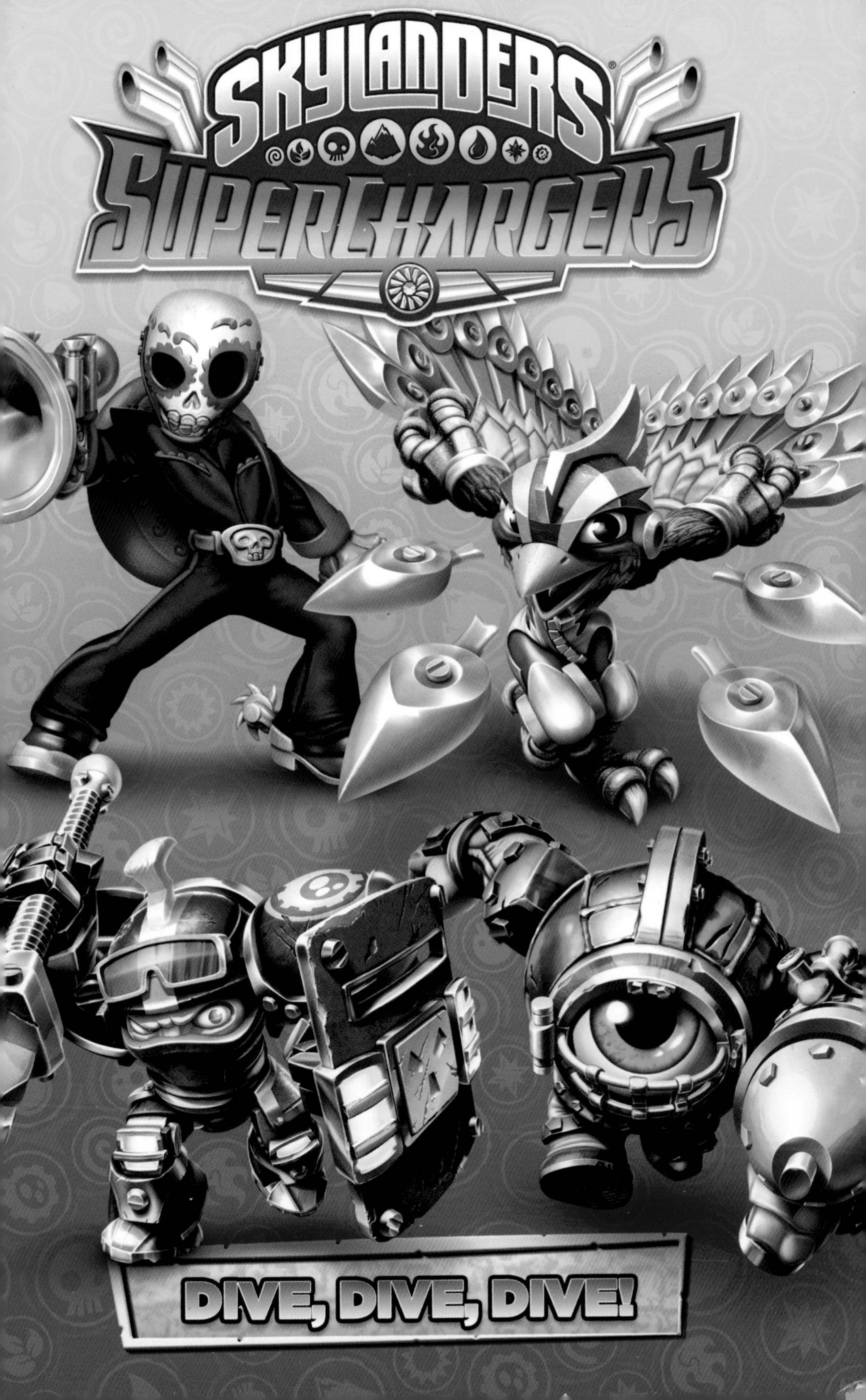

DIVE, DIVE, DIVE!

SKYLANDERS SUPERCHARGERS

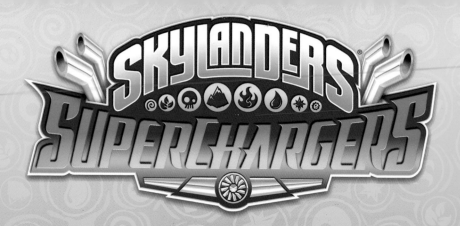

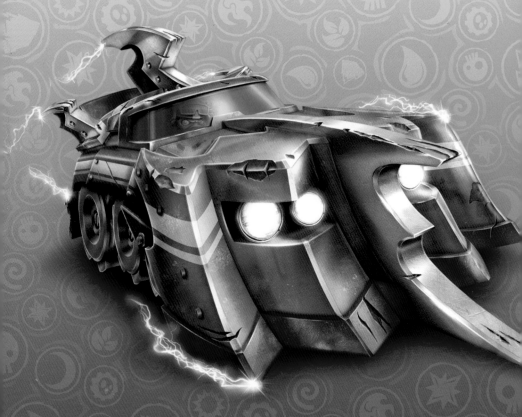

Cover Artist: **Rob Duenas**
Series Edits: **David Hedgecock**
Collection Edits: **Justin Eisinger & Alonzo Simon**
Publisher: **Ted Adams**
Collection Production: **Chris Mowry**

For international rig
please contact **licensing@idwpublishing.c**

ISBN: 978-1-63140-710-9

19 18 17 16 1 2 3

IDW
www.IDWPUBLISHING.com
ACTIVISION

Ted Adams, CEO & Publisher
Greg Goldstein, President & COO
Robbie Robbins, EVP/Sr. Graphic Artist
Chris Ryall, Chief Creative Officer/Editor-in-Chief
Laurie Windrow, Senior Vice President of Sales & Marketing
Matthew Ruzicka, CPA, Chief Financial Officer
Dirk Wood, VP of Marketing
Lorelei Bunjes, VP of Digital Services
Jeff Webber, VP of Licensing, Digital and Subsidiary Rights
Jerry Bennington, VP of New Product Development

Facebook: **facebook.com/idwpublishing**
Twitter: **@idwpublishing**
YouTube: **youtube.com/idwpublishing**
Tumblr: **tumblr.idwpublishing.com**
Instagram: **instagram.com/idwpublishing**

Originally published as SKYLANDERS SUPERCHARGERS issues #4–6.

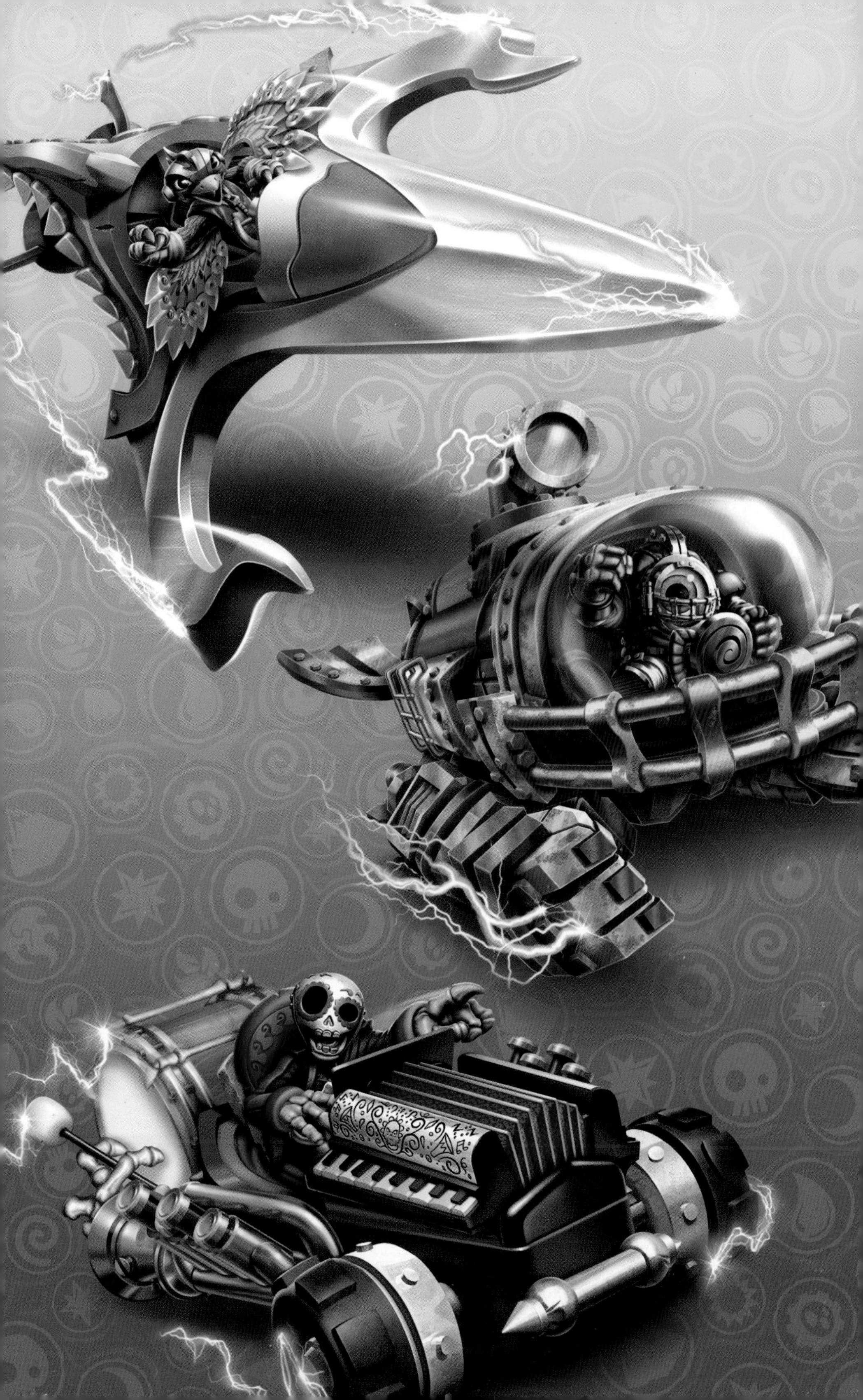

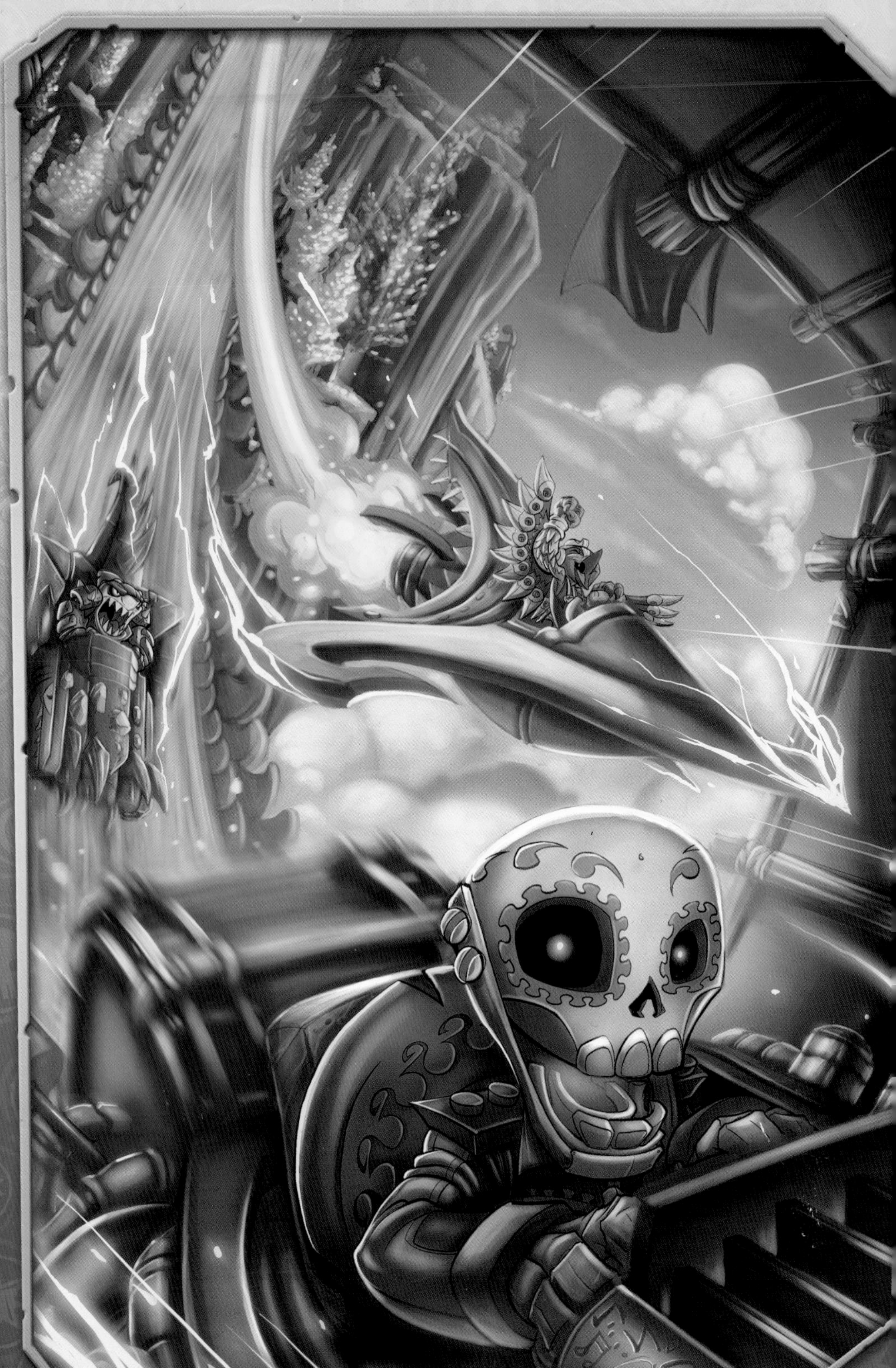

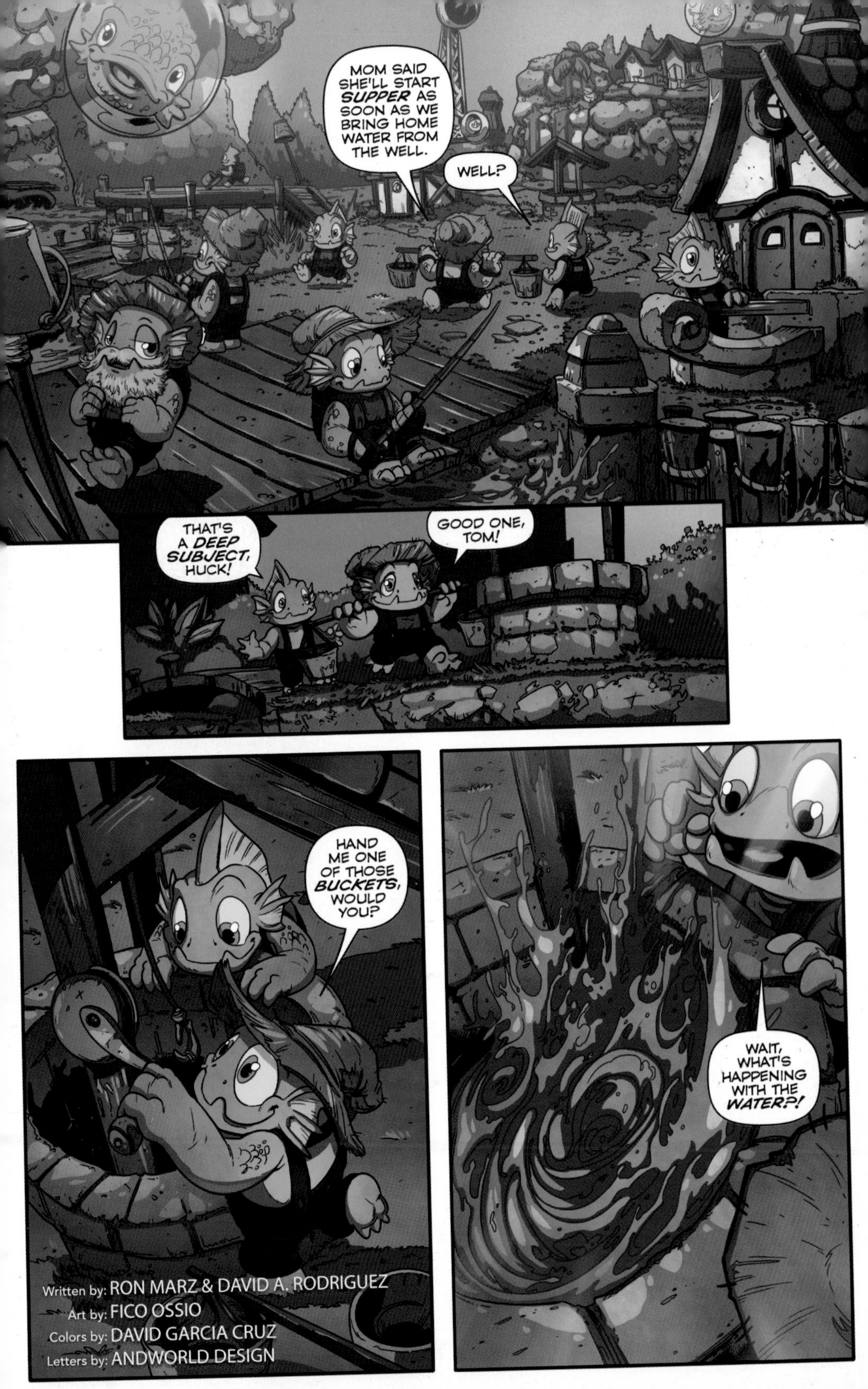
MOM SAID SHE'LL START SUPPER AS SOON AS WE BRING HOME WATER FROM THE WELL.
WELL?
THAT'S A DEEP SUBJECT, HUCK!
GOOD ONE, TOM!
HAND ME ONE OF THOSE BUCKETS, WOULD YOU?
WAIT, WHAT'S HAPPENING WITH THE WATER?!
Written by: RON MARZ & DAVID A. RODRIGUEZ
Art by: FICO OSSIO
Colors by: DAVID GARCIA CRUZ
Letters by: ANDWORLD DESIGN

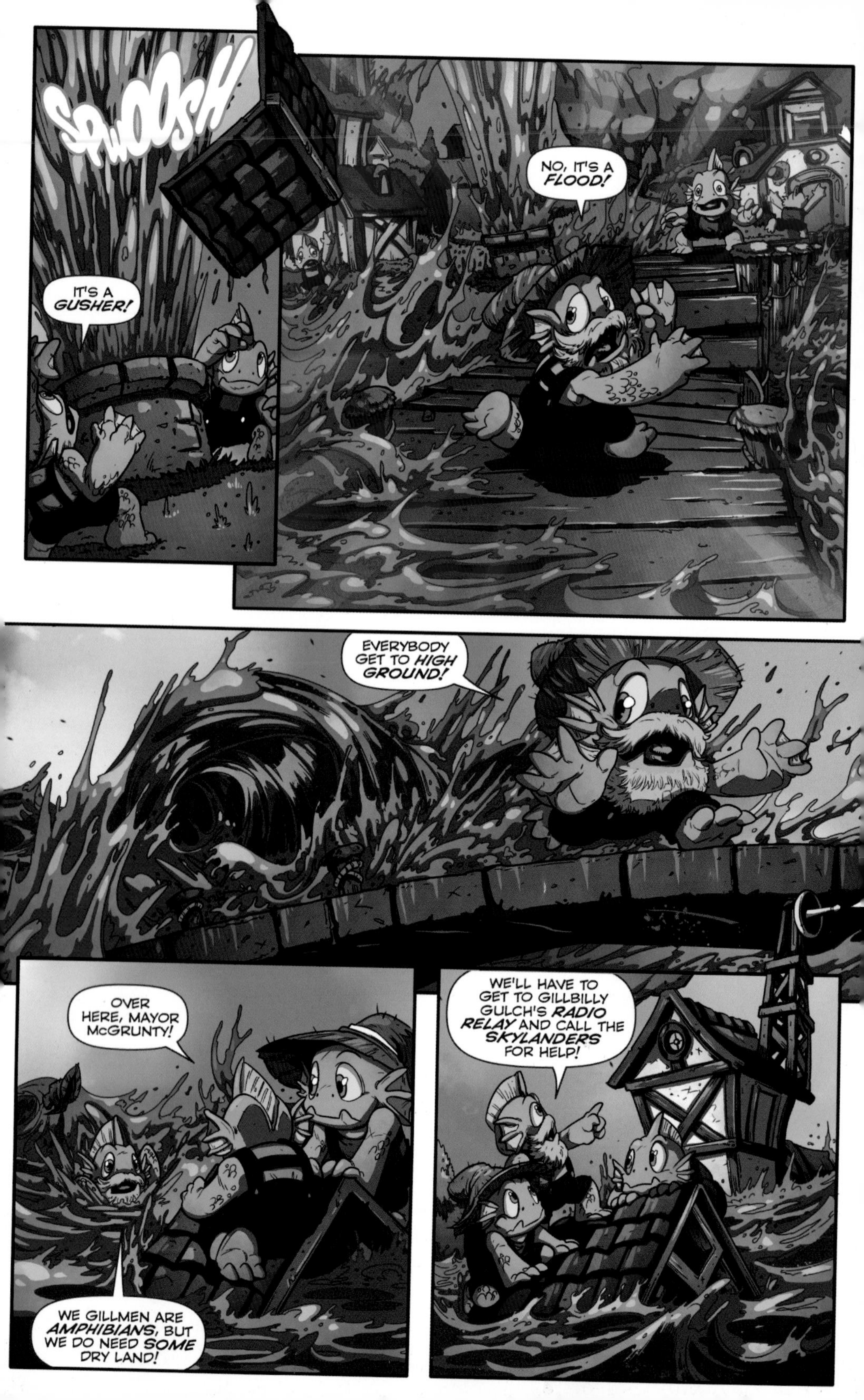
SPWOOSH!
IT'S A GUSHER!
NO, IT'S A FLOOD!
EVERYBODY GET TO HIGH GROUND!
OVER HERE, MAYOR McGRUNTY!
WE GILLMEN ARE AMPHIBIANS, BUT WE DO NEED SOME DRY LAND!
WE'LL HAVE TO GET TO GILLBILLY GULCH'S RADIO RELAY AND CALL THE SKYLANDERS FOR HELP!

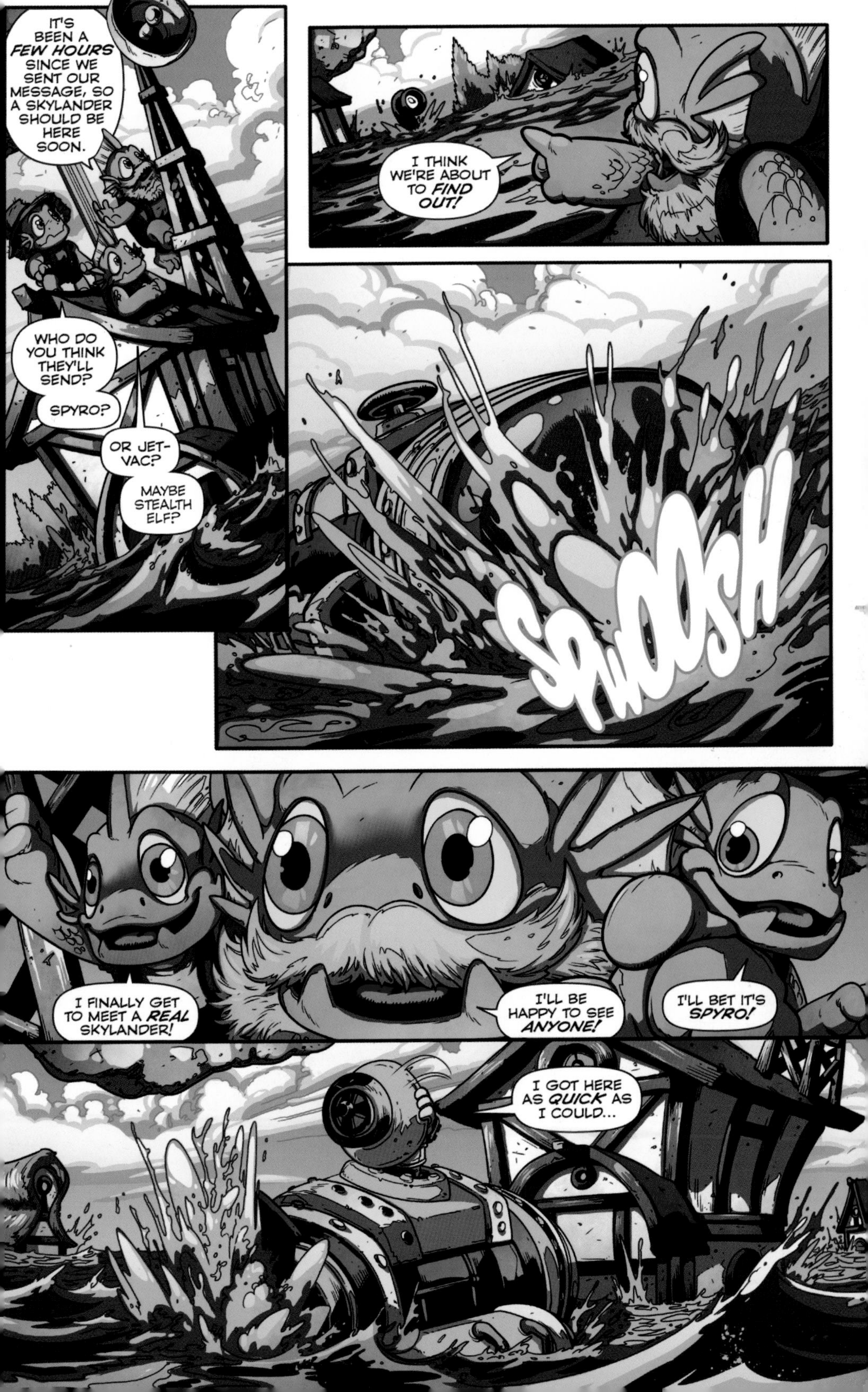
IT'S BEEN A *FEW HOURS* SINCE WE SENT OUR MESSAGE, SO A SKYLANDER SHOULD BE HERE SOON.
I THINK WE'RE ABOUT TO *FIND OUT!*
WHO DO YOU THINK THEY'LL SEND?
SPYRO?
OR JET-VAC?
MAYBE STEALTH ELF?
SPWOOSH
I FINALLY GET TO MEET A *REAL* SKYLANDER!
I'LL BE HAPPY TO SEE *ANYONE!*
I'LL BET IT'S *SPYRO!*
I GOT HERE AS *QUICK* AS I COULD...

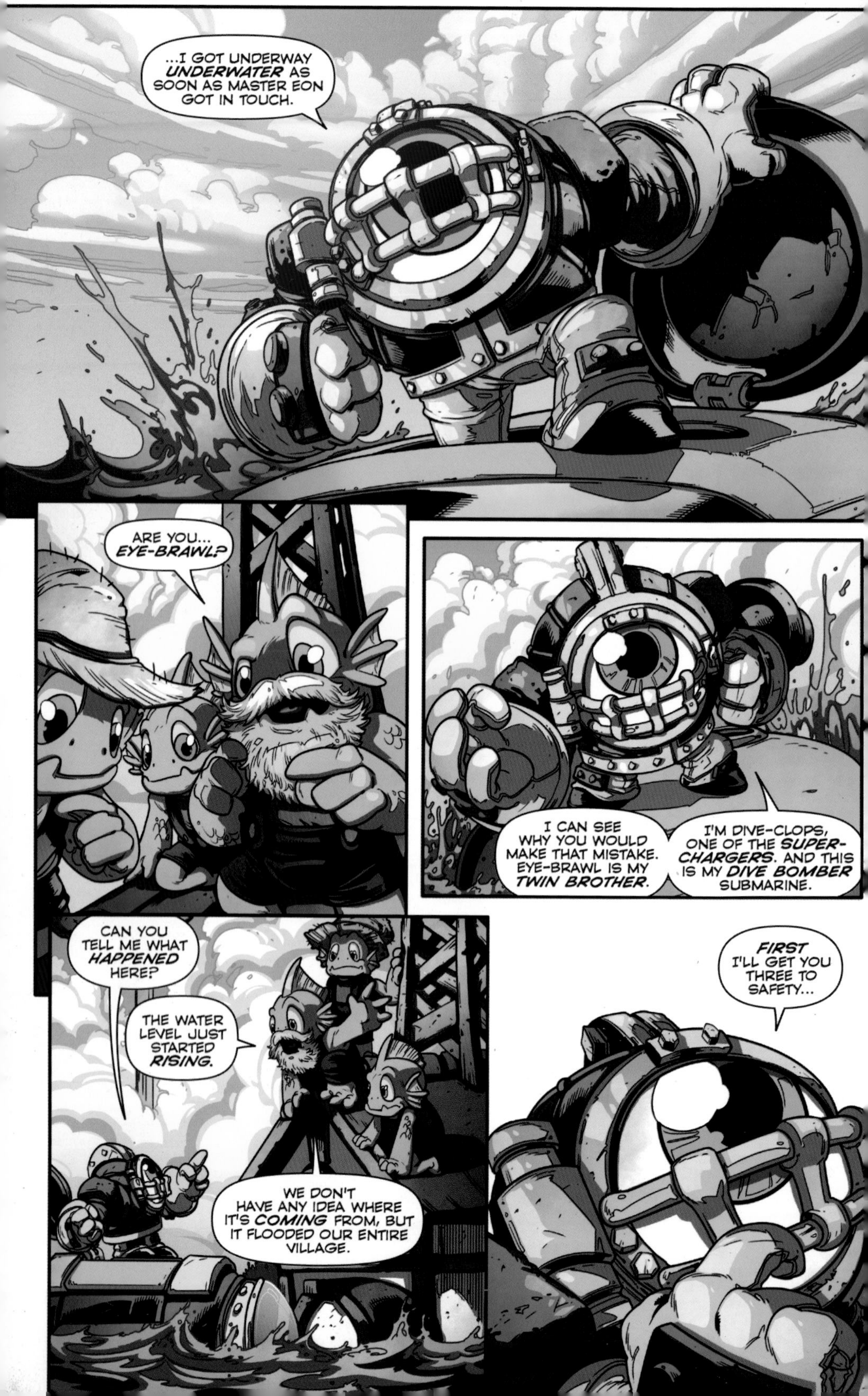

...I GOT UNDERWAY UNDERWATER AS SOON AS MASTER EON GOT IN TOUCH.
ARE YOU... EYE-BRAWL?
I CAN SEE WHY YOU WOULD MAKE THAT MISTAKE. EYE-BRAWL IS MY TWIN BROTHER.
I'M DIVE-CLOPS, ONE OF THE SUPER-CHARGERS. AND THIS IS MY DIVE BOMBER SUBMARINE.
CAN YOU TELL ME WHAT HAPPENED HERE?
THE WATER LEVEL JUST STARTED RISING.
WE DON'T HAVE ANY IDEA WHERE IT'S COMING FROM, BUT IT FLOODED OUR ENTIRE VILLAGE.
FIRST I'LL GET YOU THREE TO SAFETY...

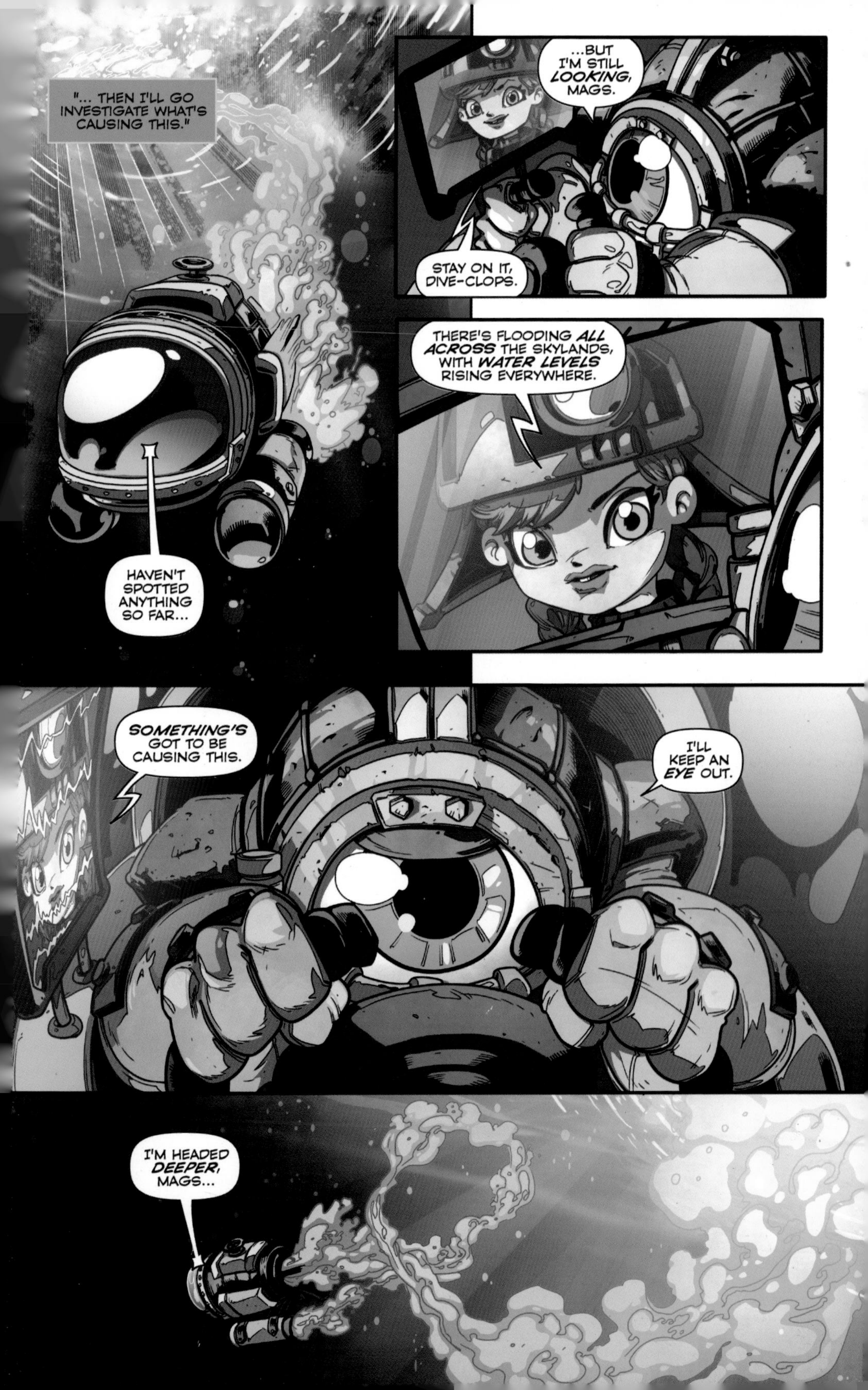
"... THEN I'LL GO INVESTIGATE WHAT'S CAUSING THIS."
HAVEN'T SPOTTED ANYTHING SO FAR...
...BUT I'M STILL LOOKING, MAGS.
STAY ON IT, DIVE-CLOPS.
THERE'S FLOODING ALL ACROSS THE SKYLANDS, WITH WATER LEVELS RISING EVERYWHERE.
SOMETHING'S GOT TO BE CAUSING THIS.
I'LL KEEP AN EYE OUT.
I'M HEADED DEEPER, MAGS...

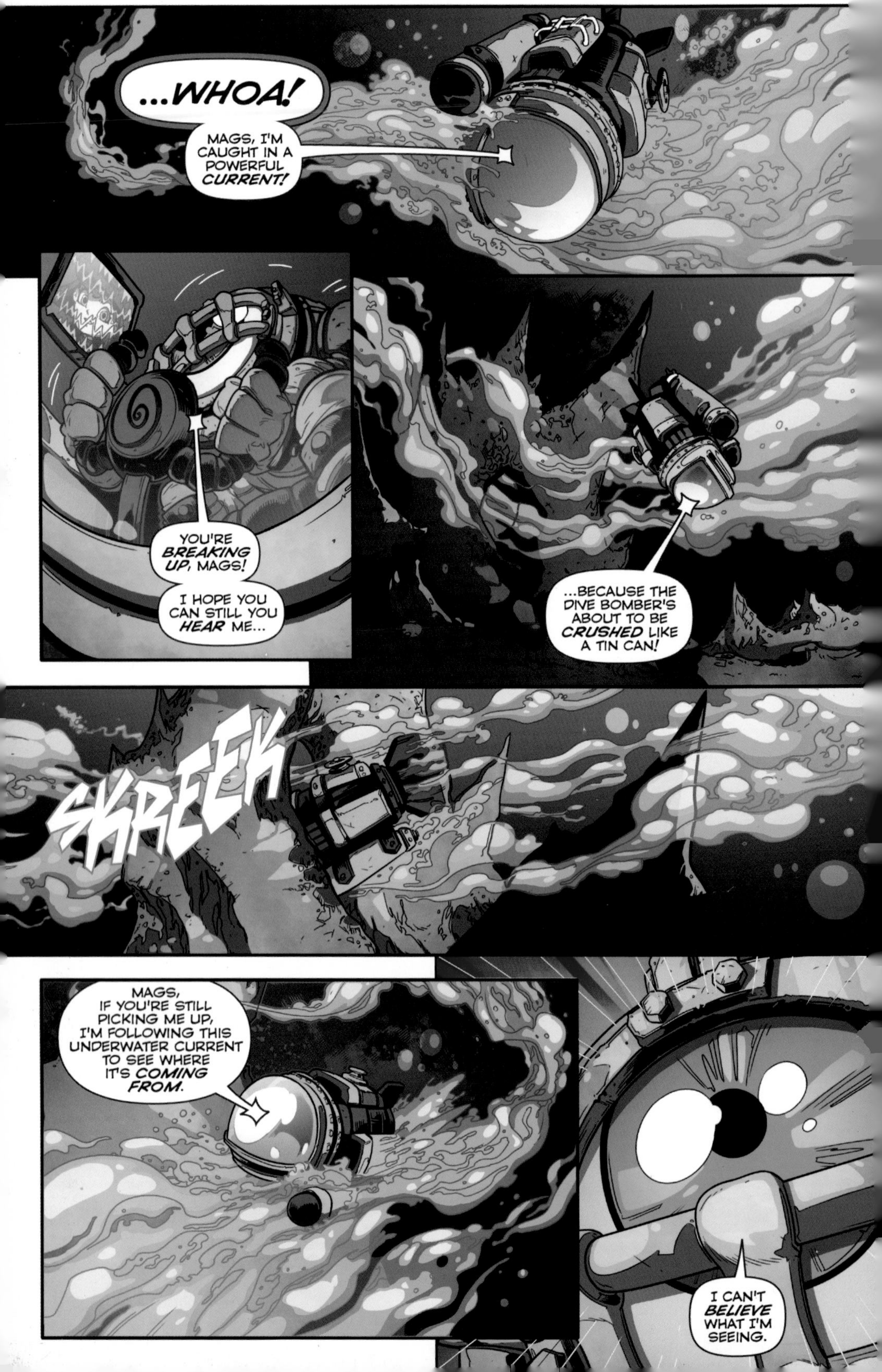
...WHOA!
MAGS, I'M CAUGHT IN A POWERFUL CURRENT!
YOU'RE BREAKING UP, MAGS!
I HOPE YOU CAN STILL YOU HEAR ME...
...BECAUSE THE DIVE BOMBER'S ABOUT TO BE CRUSHED LIKE A TIN CAN!
SKREEK
MAGS, IF YOU'RE STILL PICKING ME UP, I'M FOLLOWING THIS UNDERWATER CURRENT TO SEE WHERE IT'S COMING FROM.
I CAN'T BELIEVE WHAT I'M SEEING.

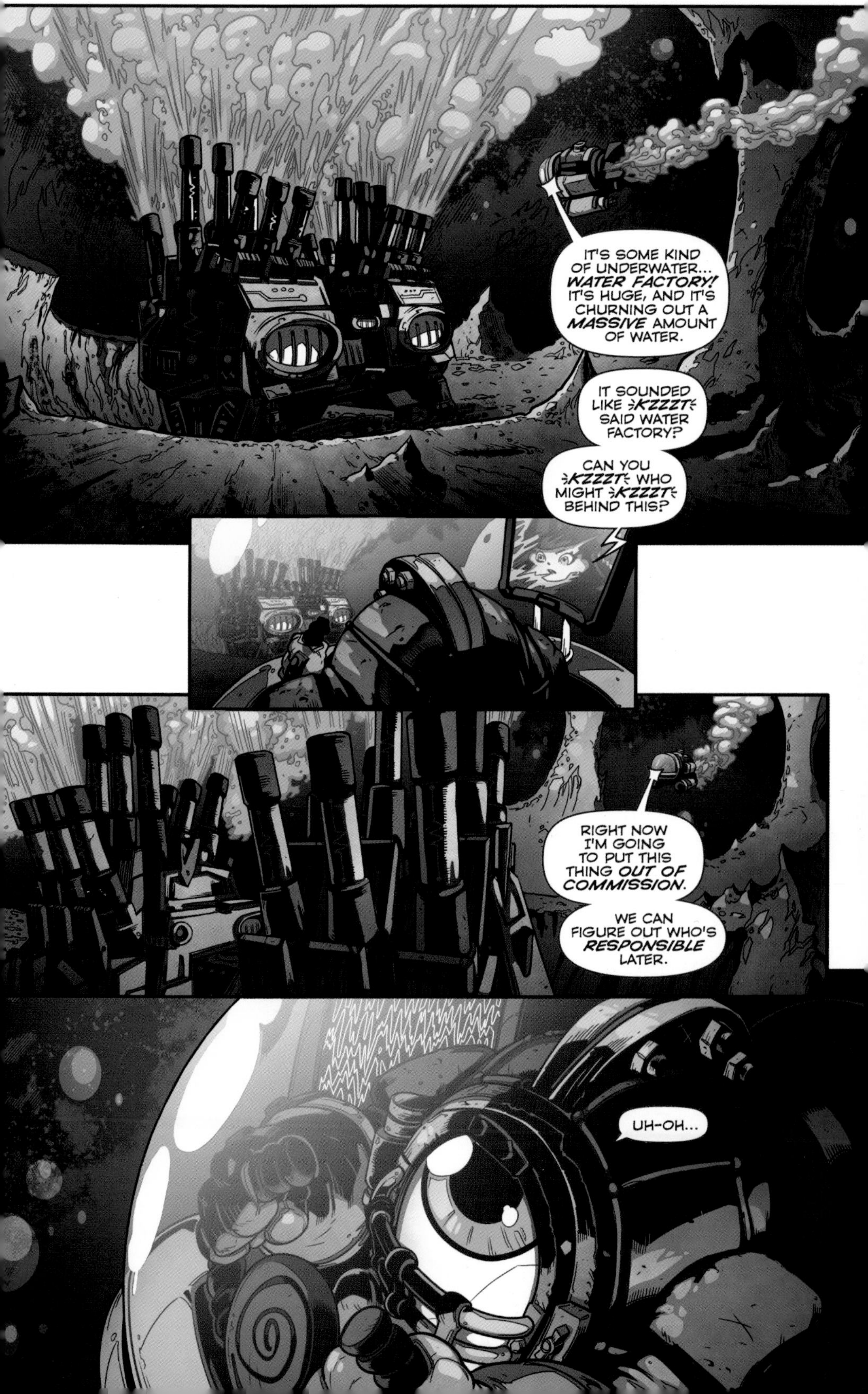
IT'S SOME KIND OF UNDERWATER... WATER FACTORY! IT'S HUGE, AND IT'S CHURNING OUT A MASSIVE AMOUNT OF WATER.
IT SOUNDED LIKE KZZZT SAID WATER FACTORY?
CAN YOU KZZZT WHO MIGHT KZZZT BEHIND THIS?
RIGHT NOW I'M GOING TO PUT THIS THING OUT OF COMMISSION.
WE CAN FIGURE OUT WHO'S RESPONSIBLE LATER.
UH-OH...

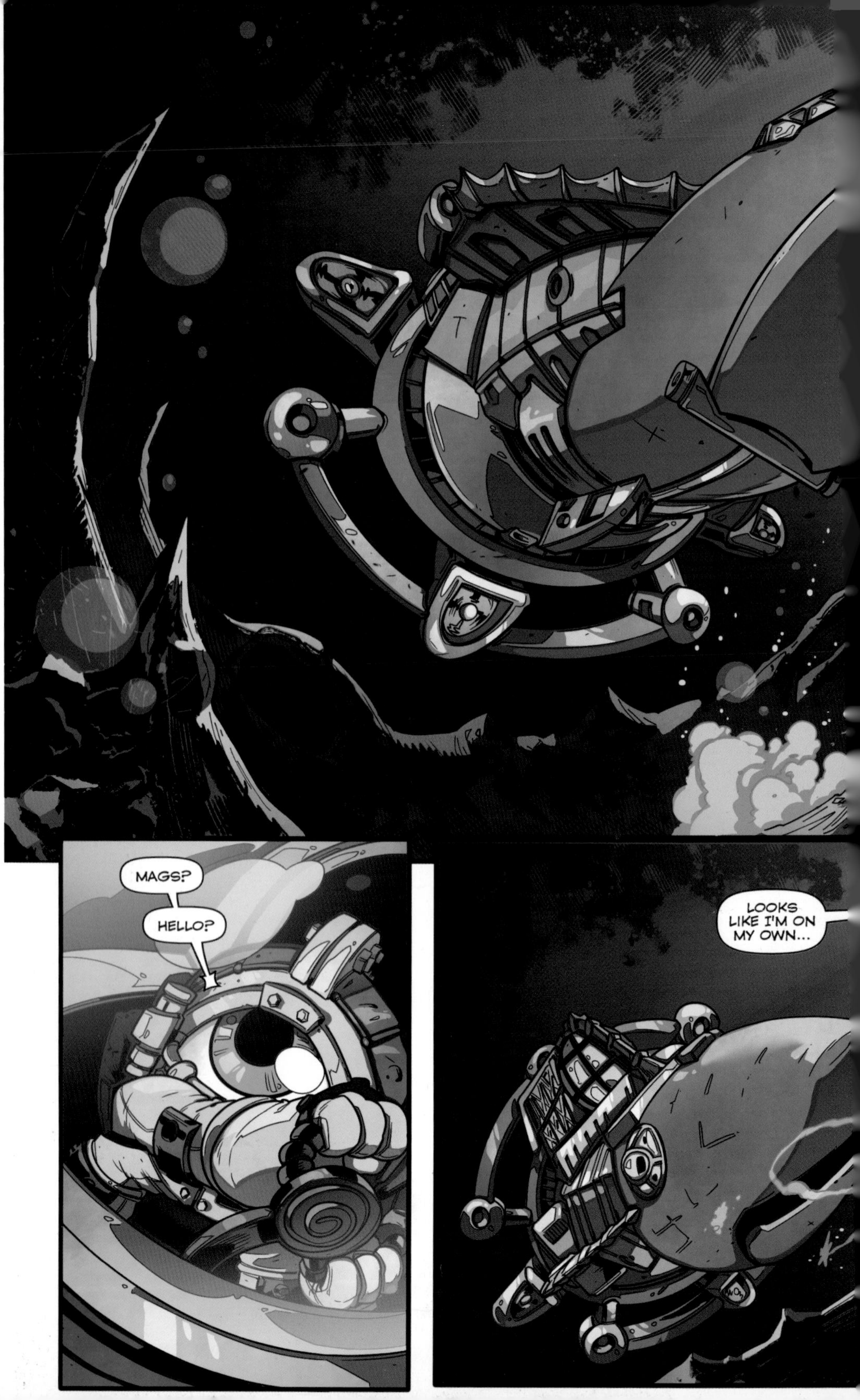
MAGS?
HELLO?
LOOKS LIKE I'M ON MY OWN...

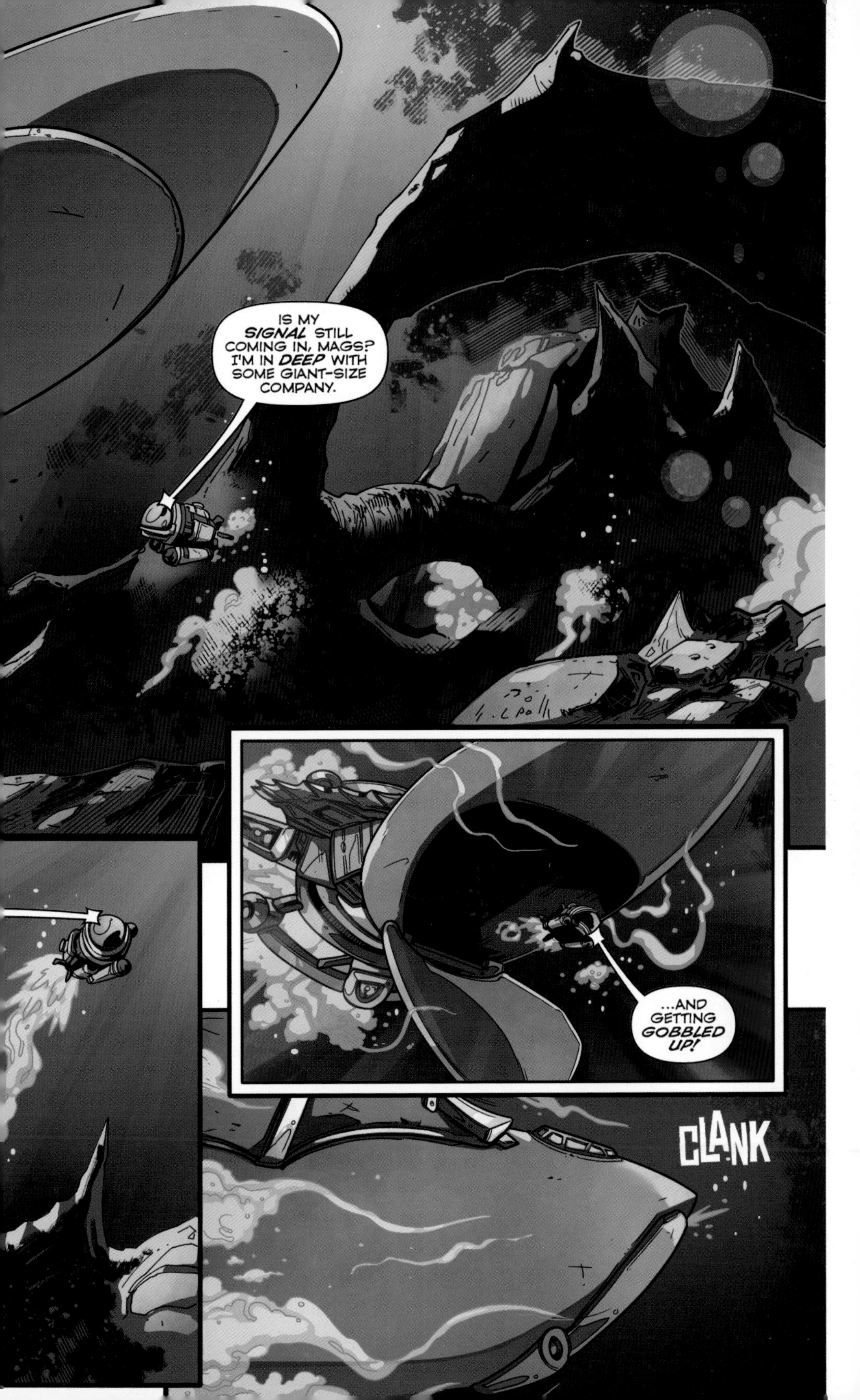
IS MY SIGNAL STILL COMING IN, MAGS? I'M IN DEEP WITH SOME GIANT-SIZE COMPANY.
...AND GETTING GOBBLED UP!
CLANK

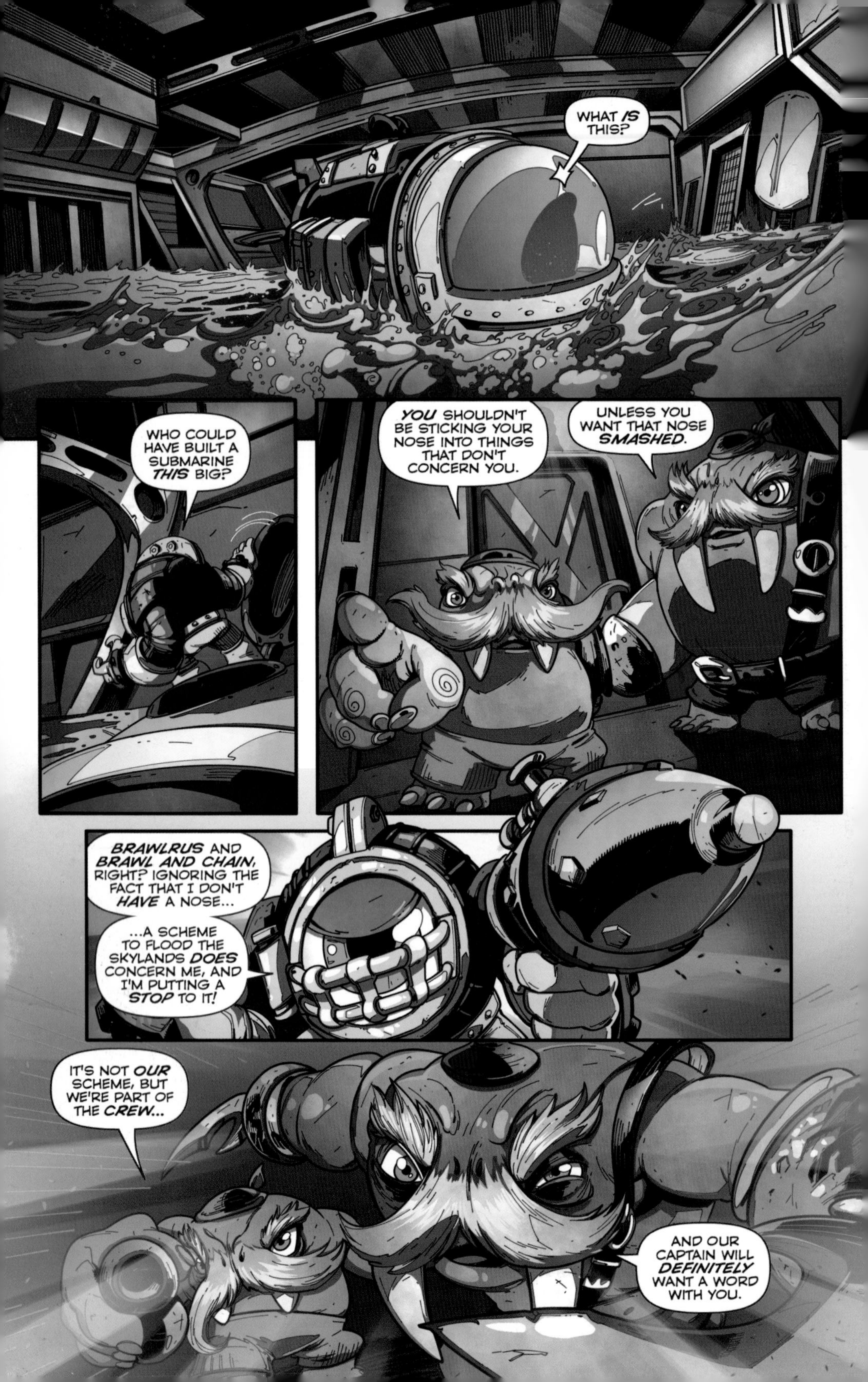

WHAT IS THIS?
WHO COULD HAVE BUILT A SUBMARINE THIS BIG?
YOU SHOULDN'T BE STICKING YOUR NOSE INTO THINGS THAT DON'T CONCERN YOU.
UNLESS YOU WANT THAT NOSE SMASHED.
BRAWLRUS AND BRAWL AND CHAIN, RIGHT? IGNORING THE FACT THAT I DON'T HAVE A NOSE...
...A SCHEME TO FLOOD THE SKYLANDS DOES CONCERN ME, AND I'M PUTTING A STOP TO IT!
IT'S NOT OUR SCHEME, BUT WE'RE PART OF THE CREW...
AND OUR CAPTAIN WILL DEFINITELY WANT A WORD WITH YOU.

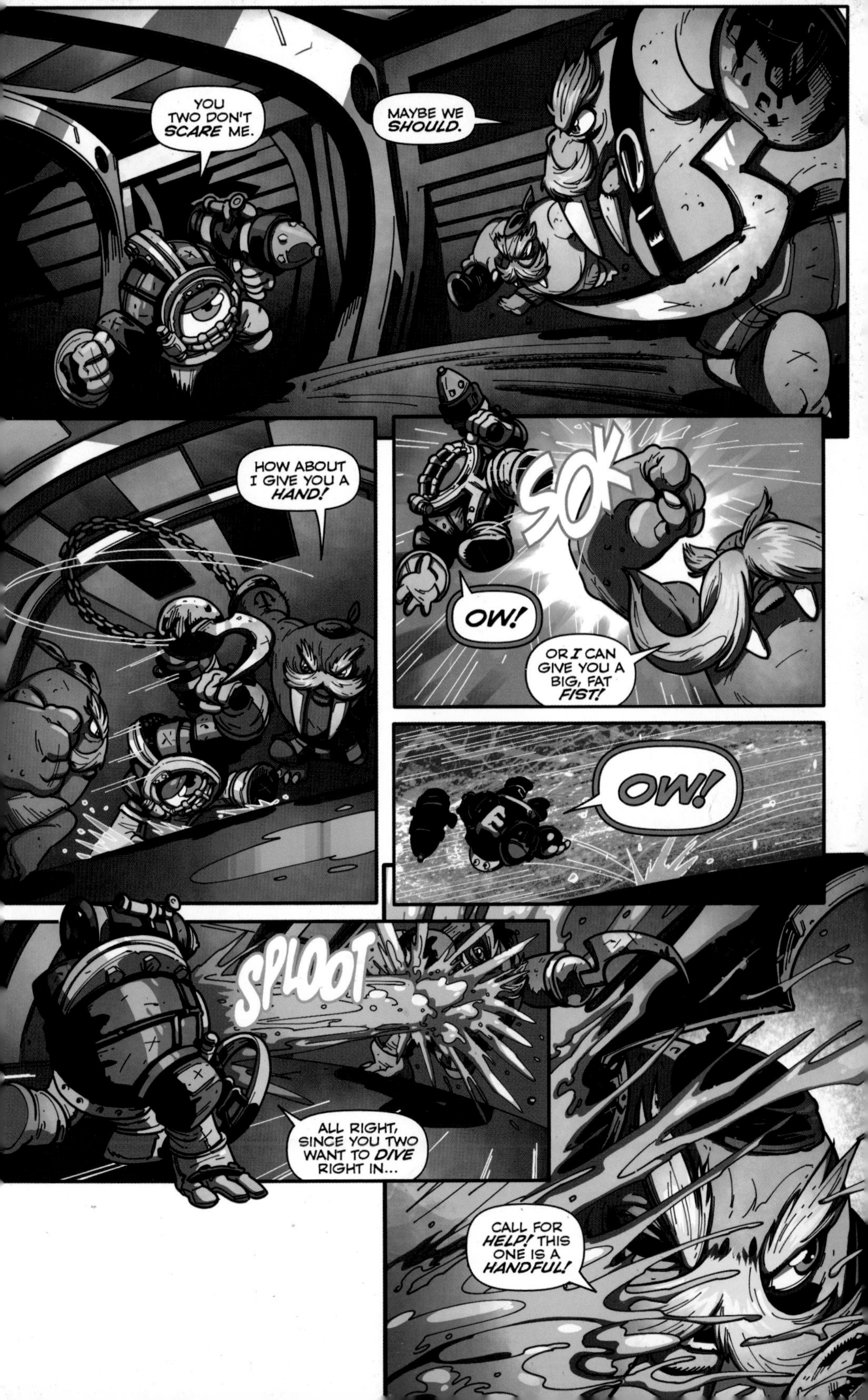
YOU TWO DON'T SCARE ME.
MAYBE WE SHOULD.
HOW ABOUT I GIVE YOU A HAND!
SOK
OW!
OR I CAN GIVE YOU A BIG, FAT FIST!
OW!
SPLOOT
ALL RIGHT, SINCE YOU TWO WANT TO DIVE RIGHT IN...
CALL FOR HELP! THIS ONE IS A HANDFUL!

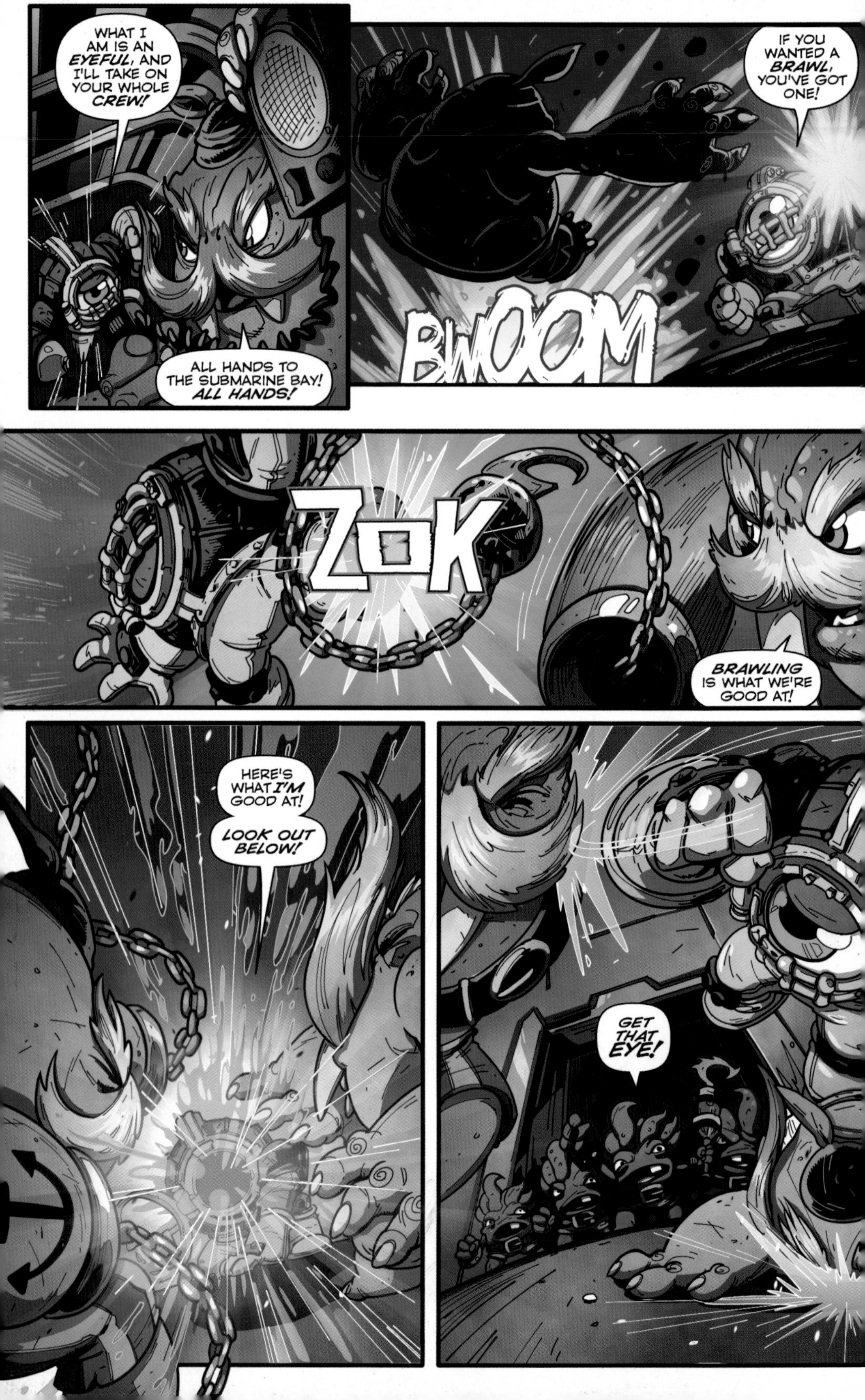

WHAT I AM IS AN EYEFUL, AND I'LL TAKE ON YOUR WHOLE CREW!
ALL HANDS TO THE SUBMARINE BAY! ALL HANDS!
IF YOU WANTED A BRAWL, YOU'VE GOT ONE!
BWOOM
ZOK
BRAWLING IS WHAT WE'RE GOOD AT!
HERE'S WHAT I'M GOOD AT!
LOOK OUT BELOW!
GET THAT EYE!

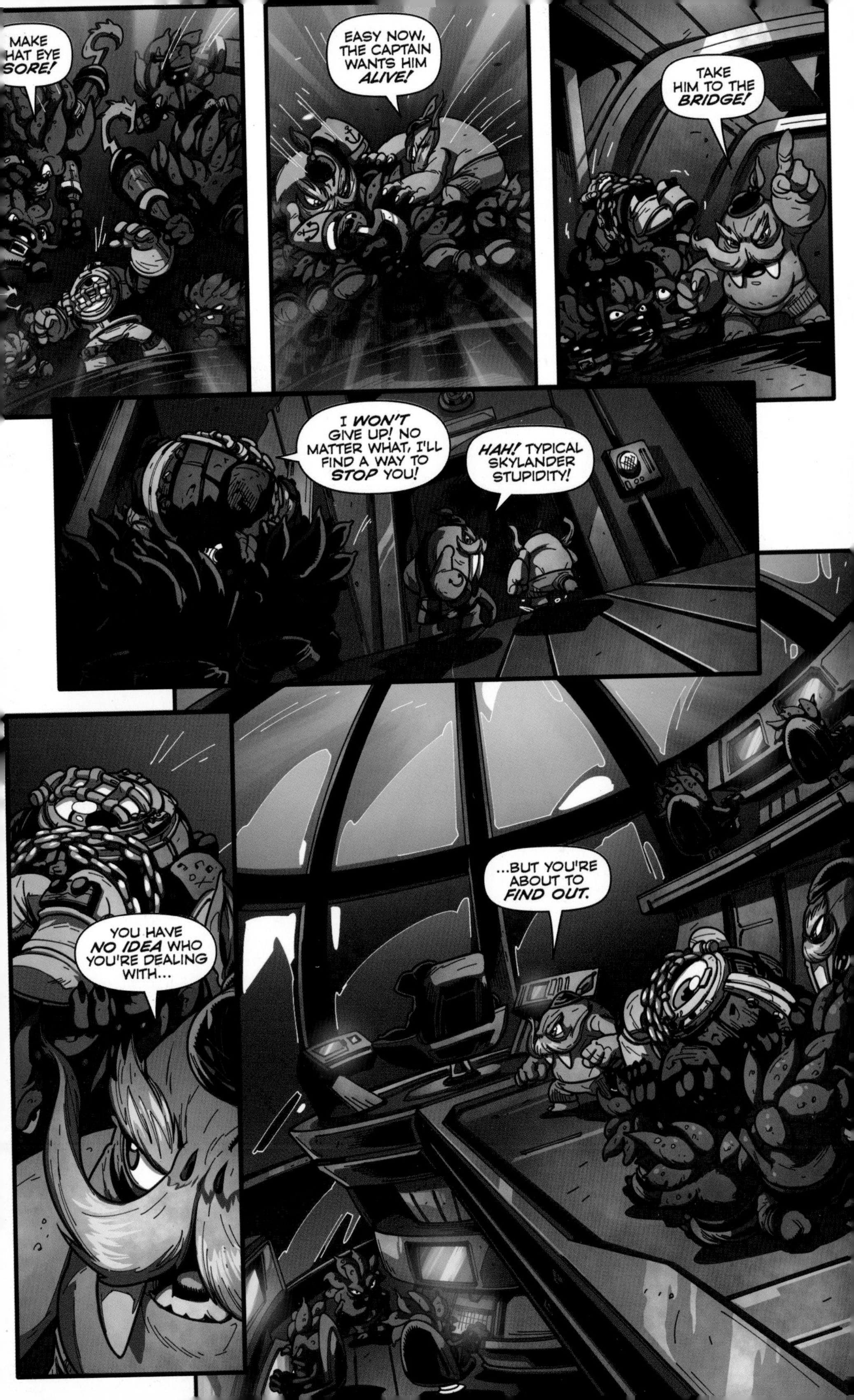
MAKE HAT EYE SORE!
EASY NOW, THE CAPTAIN WANTS HIM ALIVE!
TAKE HIM TO THE BRIDGE!
I WON'T GIVE UP! NO MATTER WHAT, I'LL FIND A WAY TO STOP YOU!
HAH! TYPICAL SKYLANDER STUPIDITY!
YOU HAVE NO IDEA WHO YOU'RE DEALING WITH...
...BUT YOU'RE ABOUT TO FIND OUT.

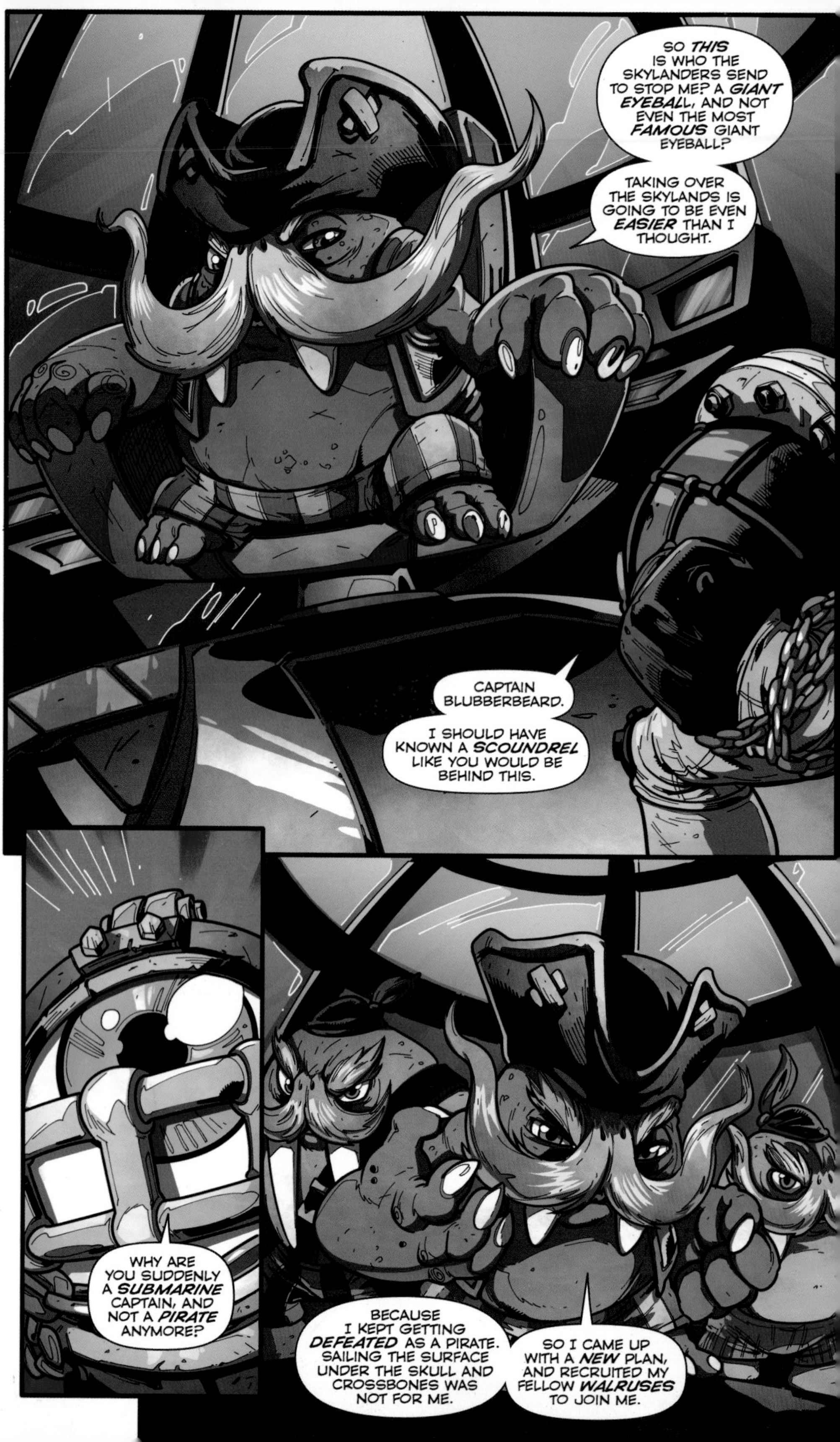
SO *THIS* IS WHO THE SKYLANDERS SEND TO STOP ME? A *GIANT EYEBALL*, AND NOT EVEN THE MOST *FAMOUS* GIANT EYEBALL?
TAKING OVER THE SKYLANDS IS GOING TO BE EVEN *EASIER* THAN I THOUGHT.
CAPTAIN BLUBBERBEARD.
I SHOULD HAVE KNOWN A *SCOUNDREL* LIKE YOU WOULD BE BEHIND THIS.
WHY ARE YOU SUDDENLY A *SUBMARINE* CAPTAIN, AND NOT A *PIRATE* ANYMORE?
BECAUSE I KEPT GETTING *DEFEATED* AS A PIRATE. SAILING THE SURFACE UNDER THE SKULL AND CROSSBONES WAS NOT FOR ME.
SO I CAME UP WITH A *NEW* PLAN, AND RECRUITED MY FELLOW *WALRUSES* TO JOIN ME.

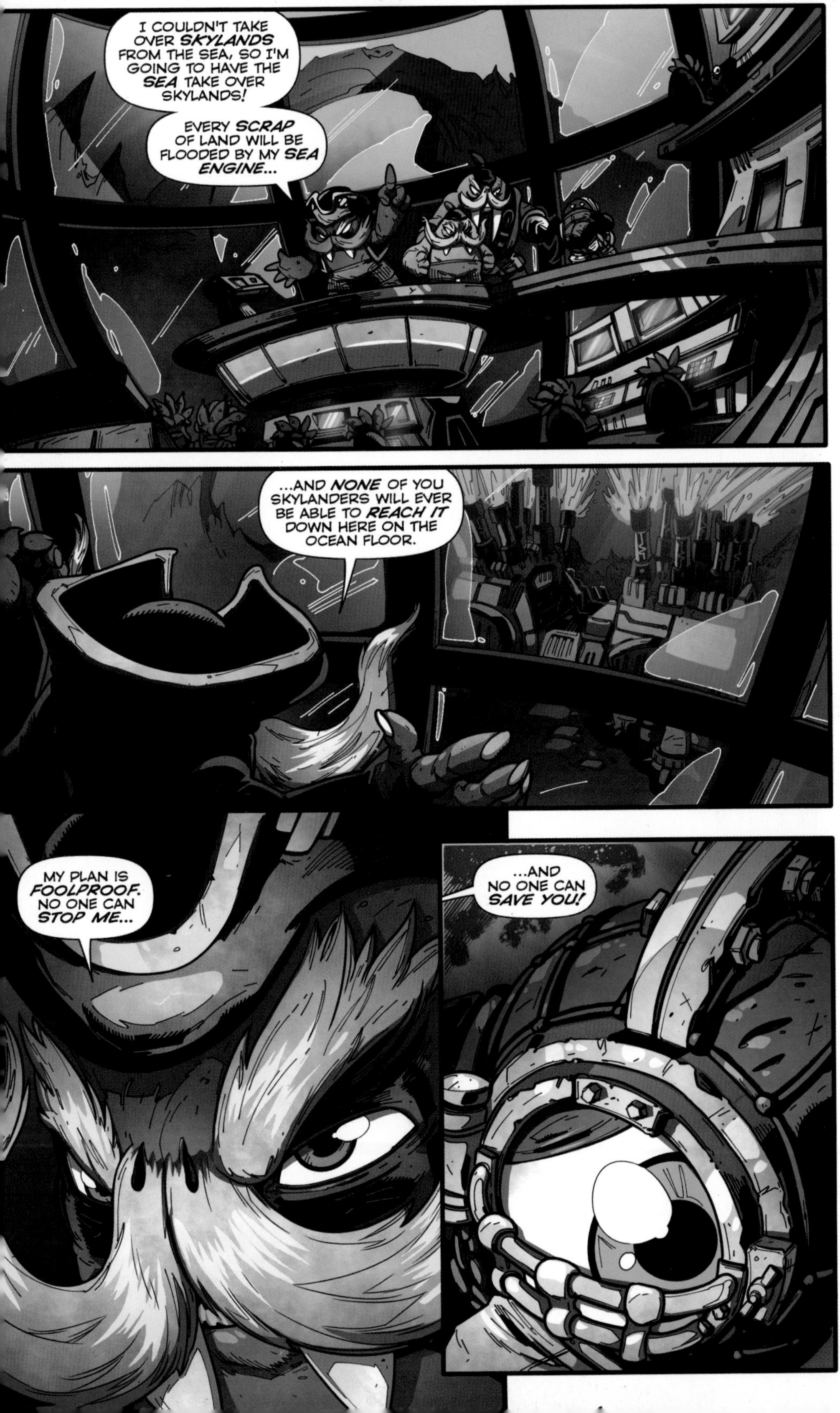
I COULDN'T TAKE OVER SKYLANDS FROM THE SEA, SO I'M GOING TO HAVE THE SEA TAKE OVER SKYLANDS!
EVERY SCRAP OF LAND WILL BE FLOODED BY MY SEA ENGINE...
...AND NONE OF YOU SKYLANDERS WILL EVER BE ABLE TO REACH IT DOWN HERE ON THE OCEAN FLOOR.
MY PLAN IS FOOLPROOF. NO ONE CAN STOP ME...
...AND NO ONE CAN SAVE YOU!

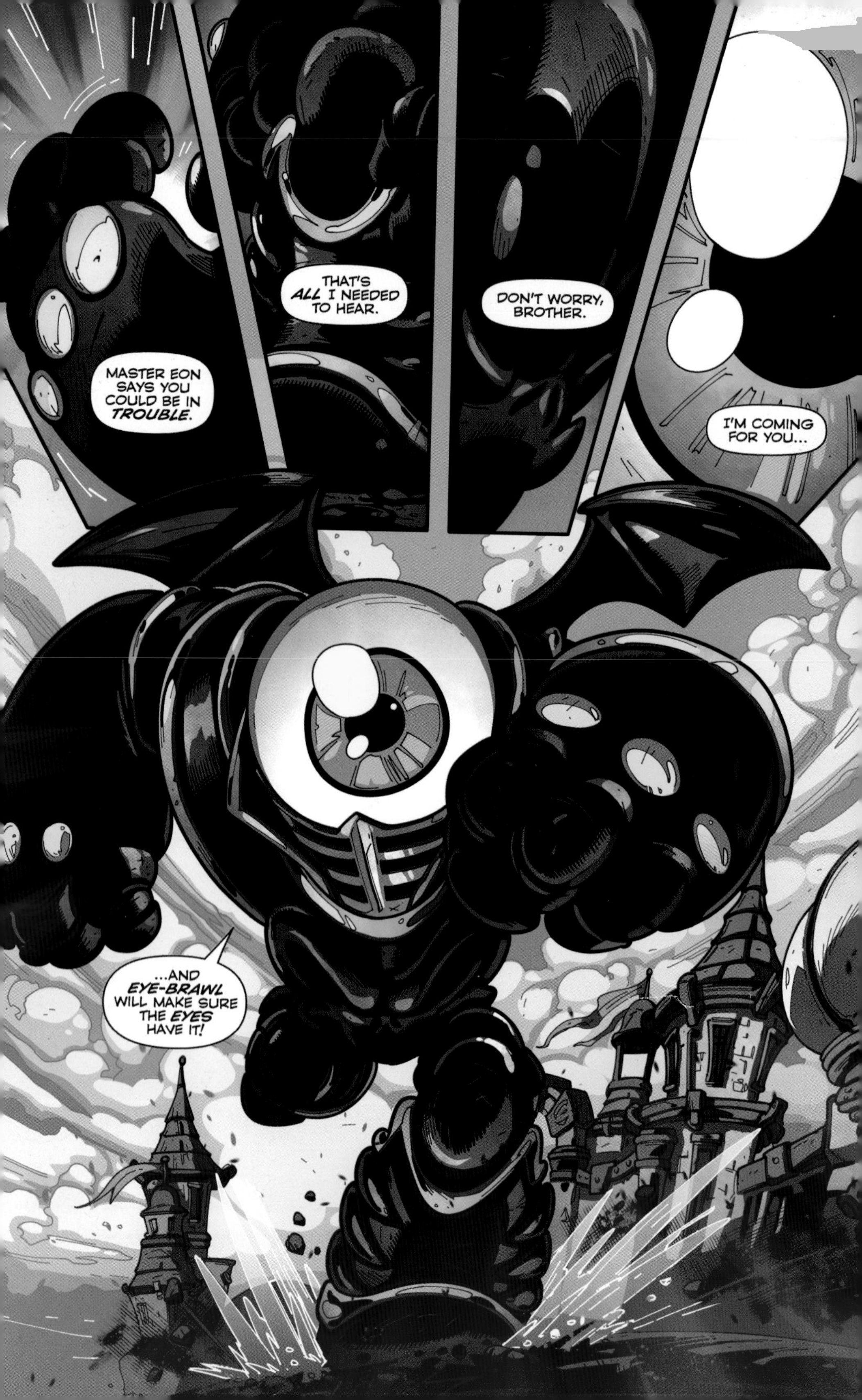
MASTER EON SAYS YOU COULD BE IN *TROUBLE*.
THAT'S *ALL* I NEEDED TO HEAR.
DON'T WORRY, BROTHER.
I'M COMING FOR YOU...
...AND *EYE-BRAWL* WILL MAKE SURE THE *EYES* HAVE IT!

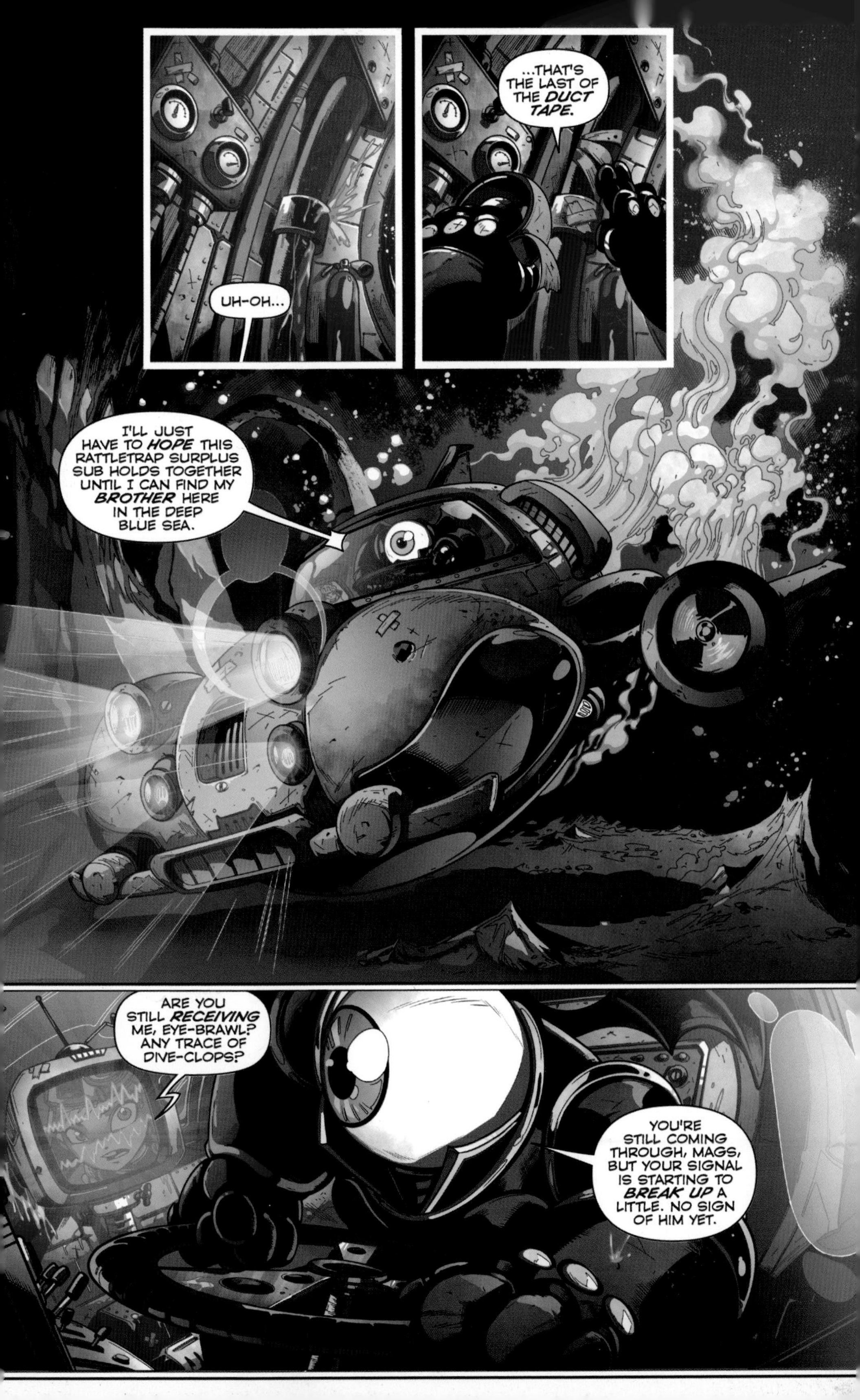
UH-OH...
...THAT'S THE LAST OF THE DUCT TAPE.
I'LL JUST HAVE TO HOPE THIS RATTLETRAP SURPLUS SUB HOLDS TOGETHER UNTIL I CAN FIND MY BROTHER HERE IN THE DEEP BLUE SEA.
ARE YOU STILL RECEIVING ME, EYE-BRAWL? ANY TRACE OF DIVE-CLOPS?
YOU'RE STILL COMING THROUGH, MAGS, BUT YOUR SIGNAL IS STARTING TO BREAK UP A LITTLE. NO SIGN OF HIM YET.

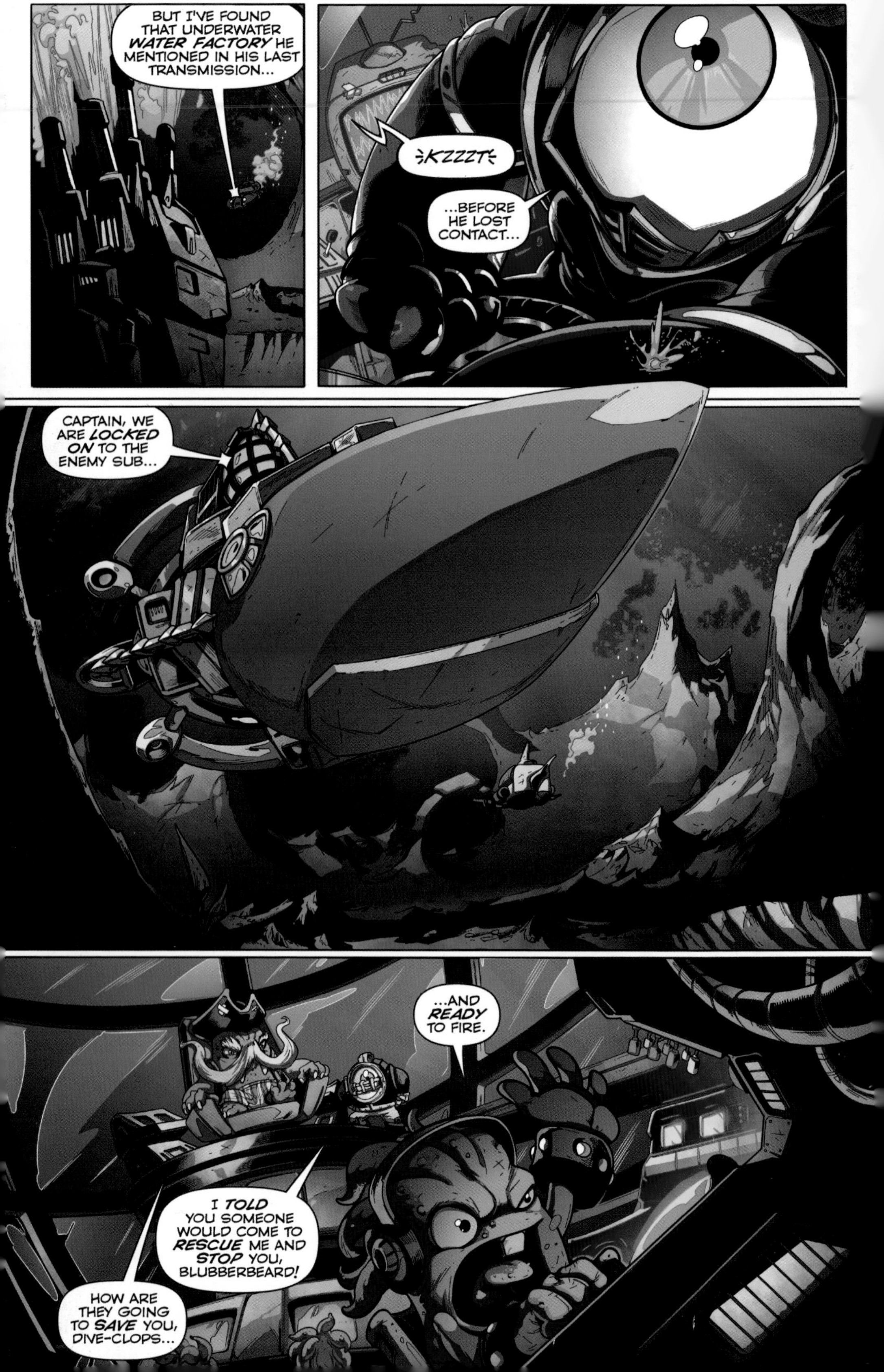
BUT I'VE FOUND THAT UNDERWATER *WATER FACTORY* HE MENTIONED IN HIS LAST TRANSMISSION...
KZZZT
...BEFORE HE LOST CONTACT...
CAPTAIN, WE ARE *LOCKED ON* TO THE ENEMY SUB...
...AND *READY* TO FIRE.
I *TOLD* YOU SOMEONE WOULD COME TO *RESCUE* ME AND *STOP* YOU, BLUBBERBEARD!
HOW ARE THEY GOING TO *SAVE* YOU, DIVE-CLOPS...

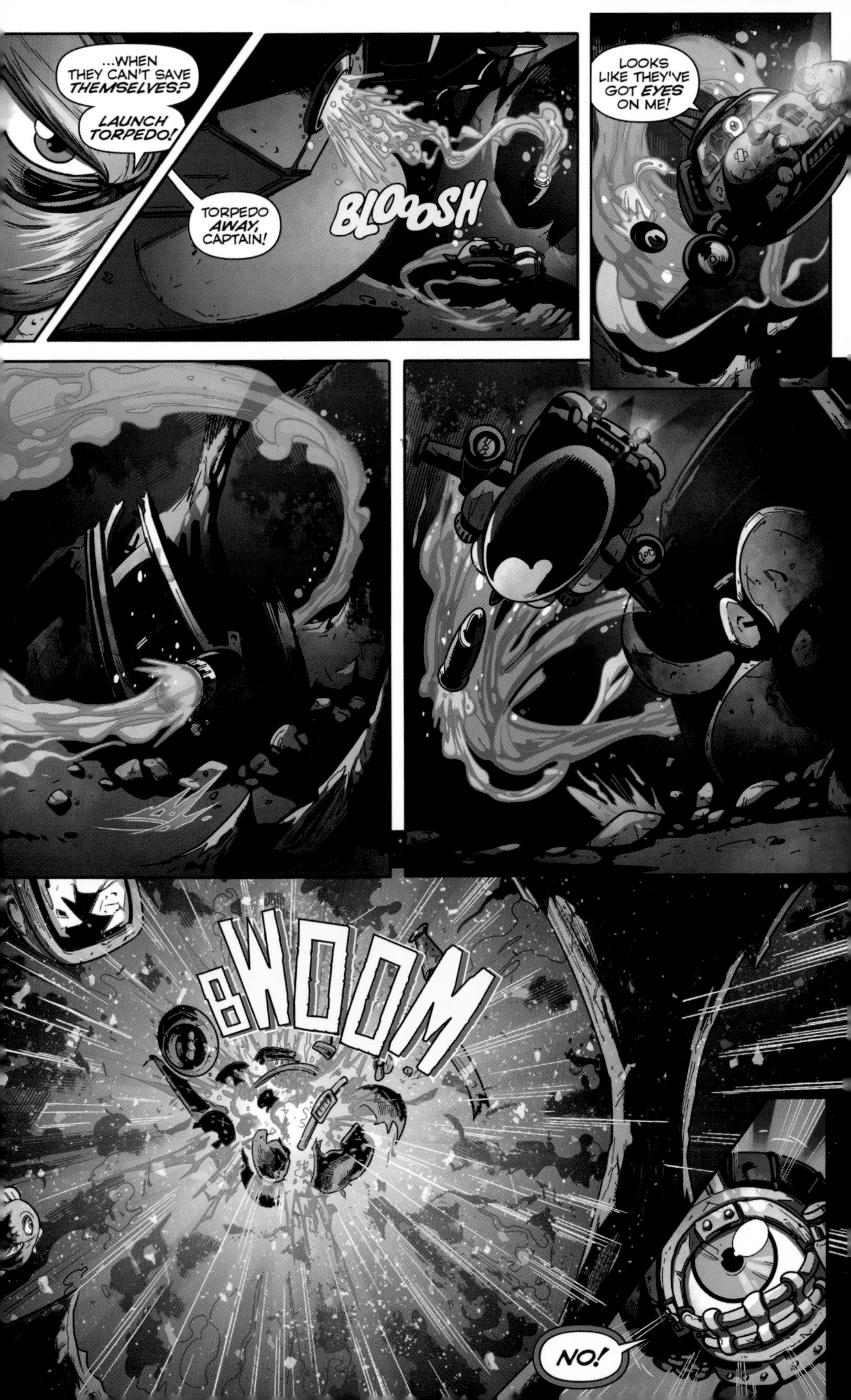
...WHEN THEY CAN'T SAVE THEMSELVES?
LAUNCH TORPEDO!
TORPEDO AWAY, CAPTAIN!
BLOOOSH
LOOKS LIKE THEY'VE GOT EYES ON ME!
BWOOM
NO!

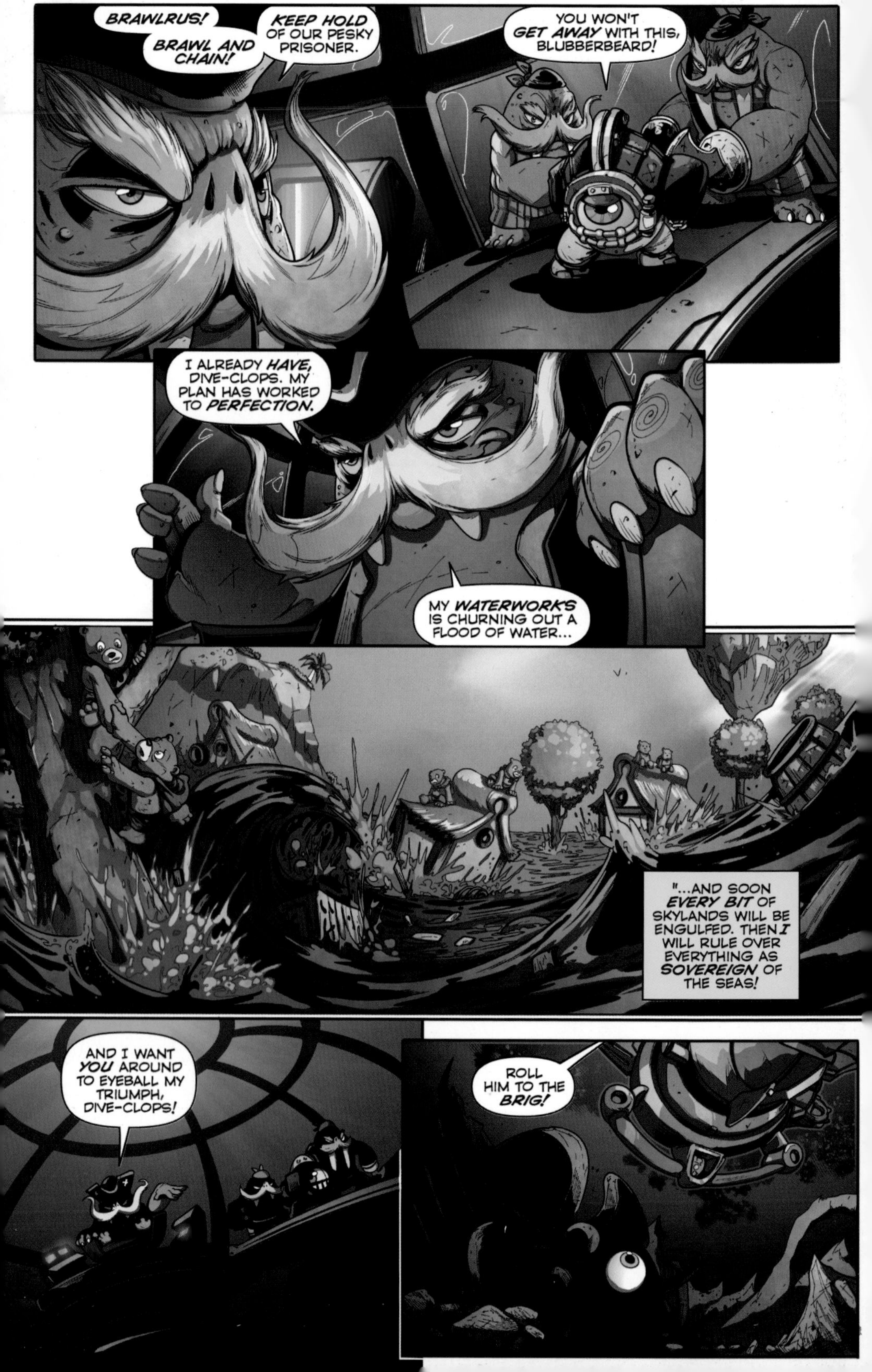
BRAWLRUS!
BRAWL AND CHAIN!
KEEP HOLD OF OUR PESKY PRISONER.
YOU WON'T GET AWAY WITH THIS, BLUBBERBEARD!
I ALREADY HAVE, DIVE-CLOPS. MY PLAN HAS WORKED TO PERFECTION.
MY WATERWORKS IS CHURNING OUT A FLOOD OF WATER...
"...AND SOON EVERY BIT OF SKYLANDS WILL BE ENGULFED. THEN I WILL RULE OVER EVERYTHING AS SOVEREIGN OF THE SEAS!
AND I WANT YOU AROUND TO EYEBALL MY TRIUMPH, DIVE-CLOPS!
ROLL HIM TO THE BRIG!

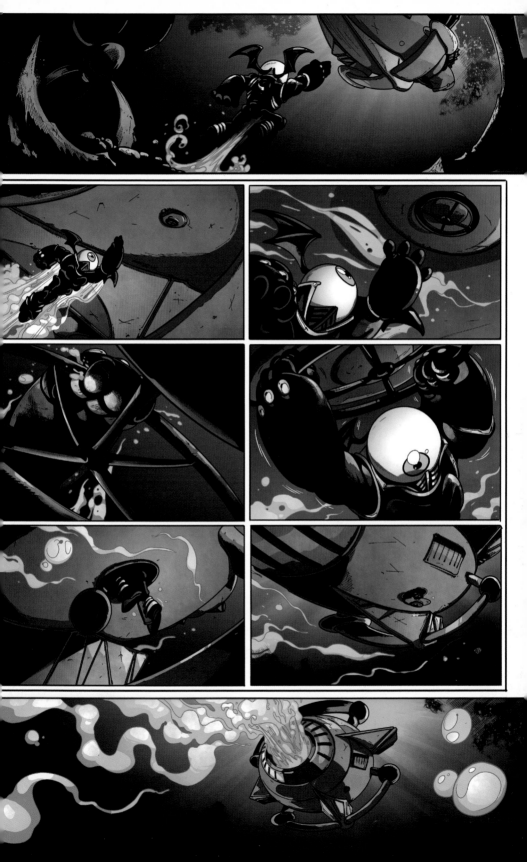

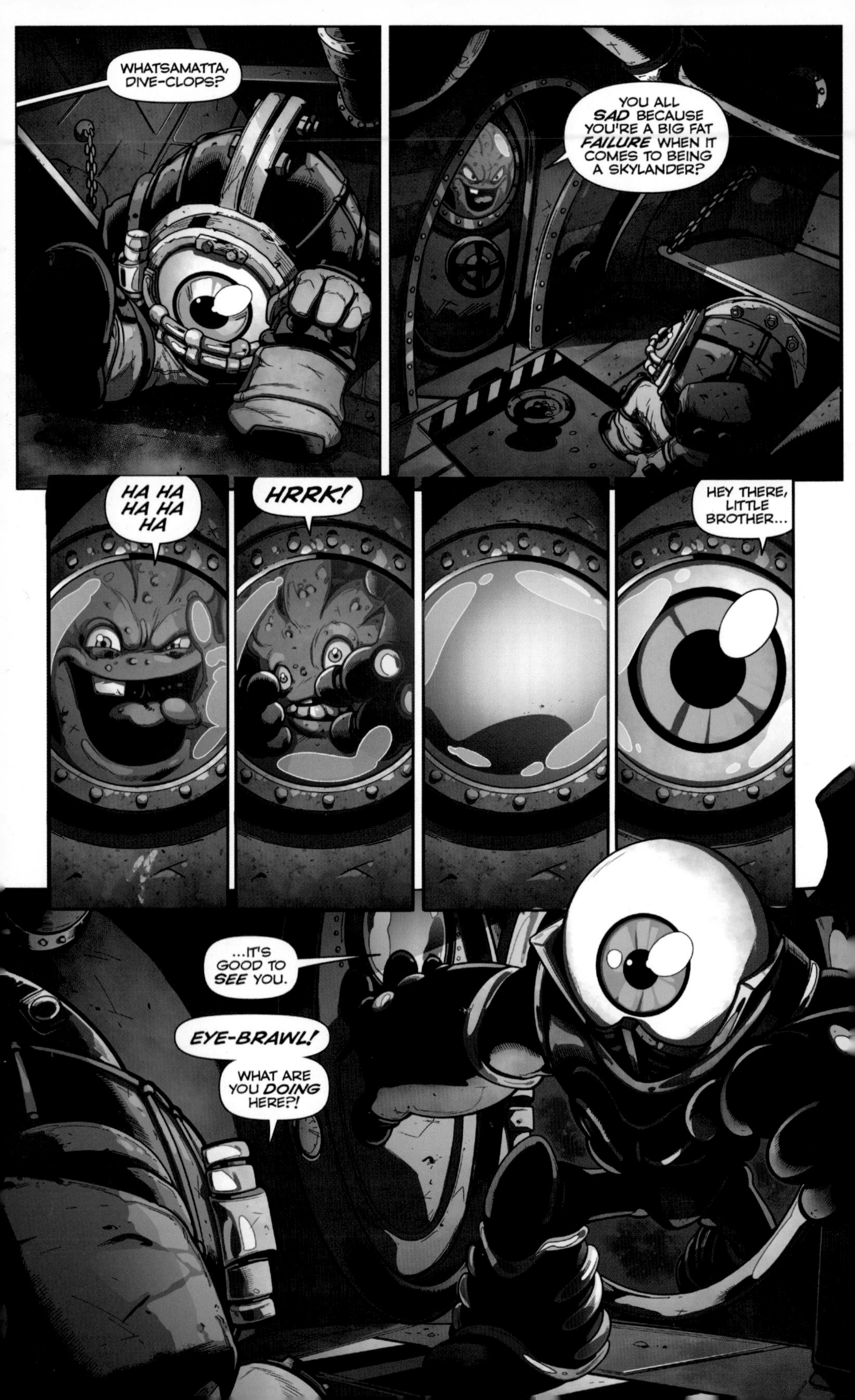
WHATSAMATTA, DIVE-CLOPS?
YOU ALL SAD BECAUSE YOU'RE A BIG FAT FAILURE WHEN IT COMES TO BEING A SKYLANDER?
HA HA HA HA HA
HRRK!
HEY THERE, LITTLE BROTHER...
...IT'S GOOD TO SEE YOU.
EYE-BRAWL!
WHAT ARE YOU DOING HERE?!

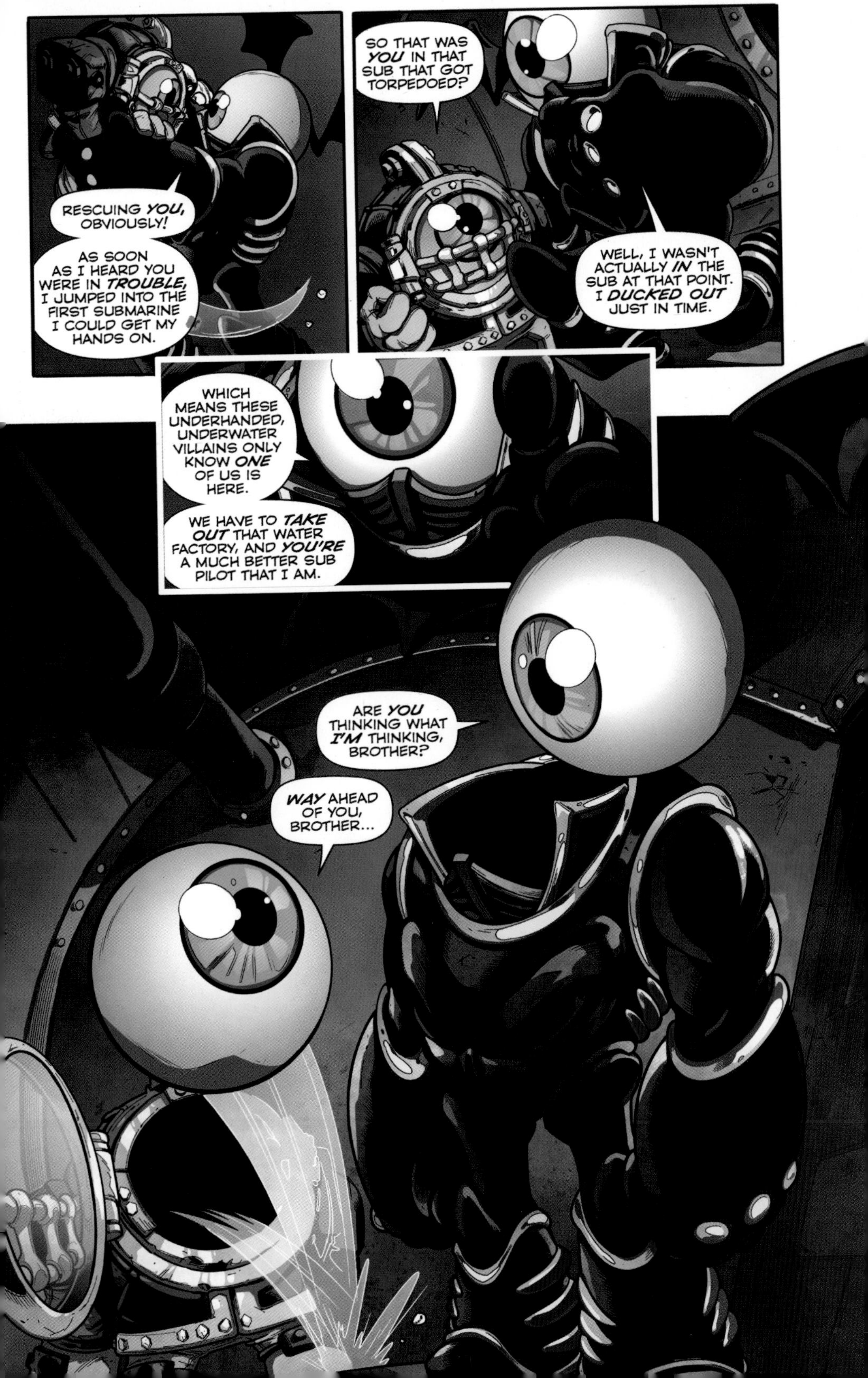
RESCUING YOU, OBVIOUSLY!
AS SOON AS I HEARD YOU WERE IN TROUBLE, I JUMPED INTO THE FIRST SUBMARINE I COULD GET MY HANDS ON.
SO THAT WAS YOU IN THAT SUB THAT GOT TORPEDOED?
WELL, I WASN'T ACTUALLY IN THE SUB AT THAT POINT. I DUCKED OUT JUST IN TIME.
WHICH MEANS THESE UNDERHANDED, UNDERWATER VILLAINS ONLY KNOW ONE OF US IS HERE.
WE HAVE TO TAKE OUT THAT WATER FACTORY, AND YOU'RE A MUCH BETTER SUB PILOT THAT I AM.
ARE YOU THINKING WHAT I'M THINKING, BROTHER?
WAY AHEAD OF YOU, BROTHER...

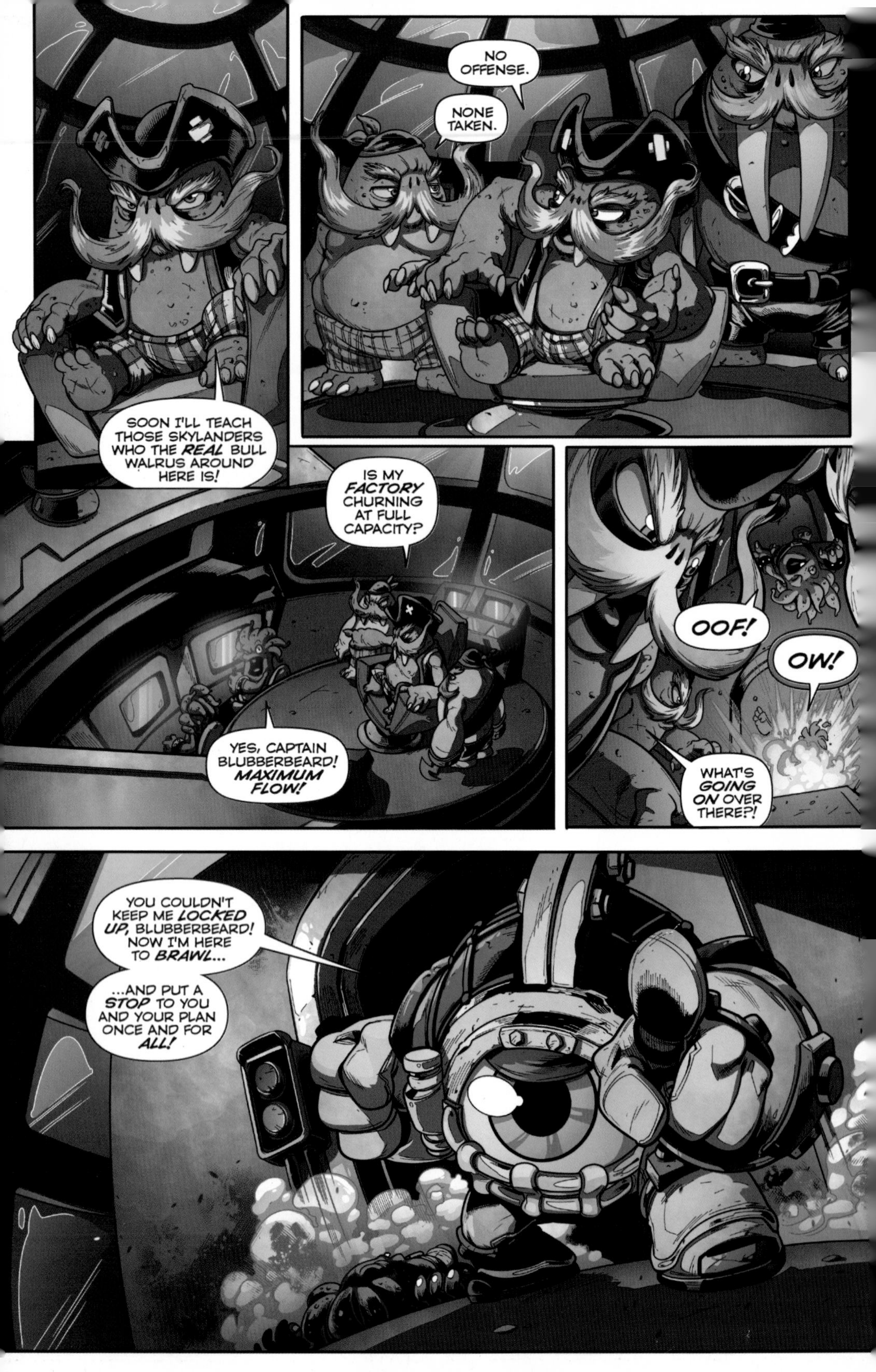
SOON I'LL TEACH THOSE SKYLANDERS WHO THE REAL BULL WALRUS AROUND HERE IS!
NO OFFENSE.
NONE TAKEN.
IS MY FACTORY CHURNING AT FULL CAPACITY?
YES, CAPTAIN BLUBBERBEARD! MAXIMUM FLOW!
OOF!
OW!
WHAT'S GOING ON OVER THERE?!
YOU COULDN'T KEEP ME LOCKED UP, BLUBBERBEARD! NOW I'M HERE TO BRAWL...
...AND PUT A STOP TO YOU AND YOUR PLAN ONCE AND FOR ALL!

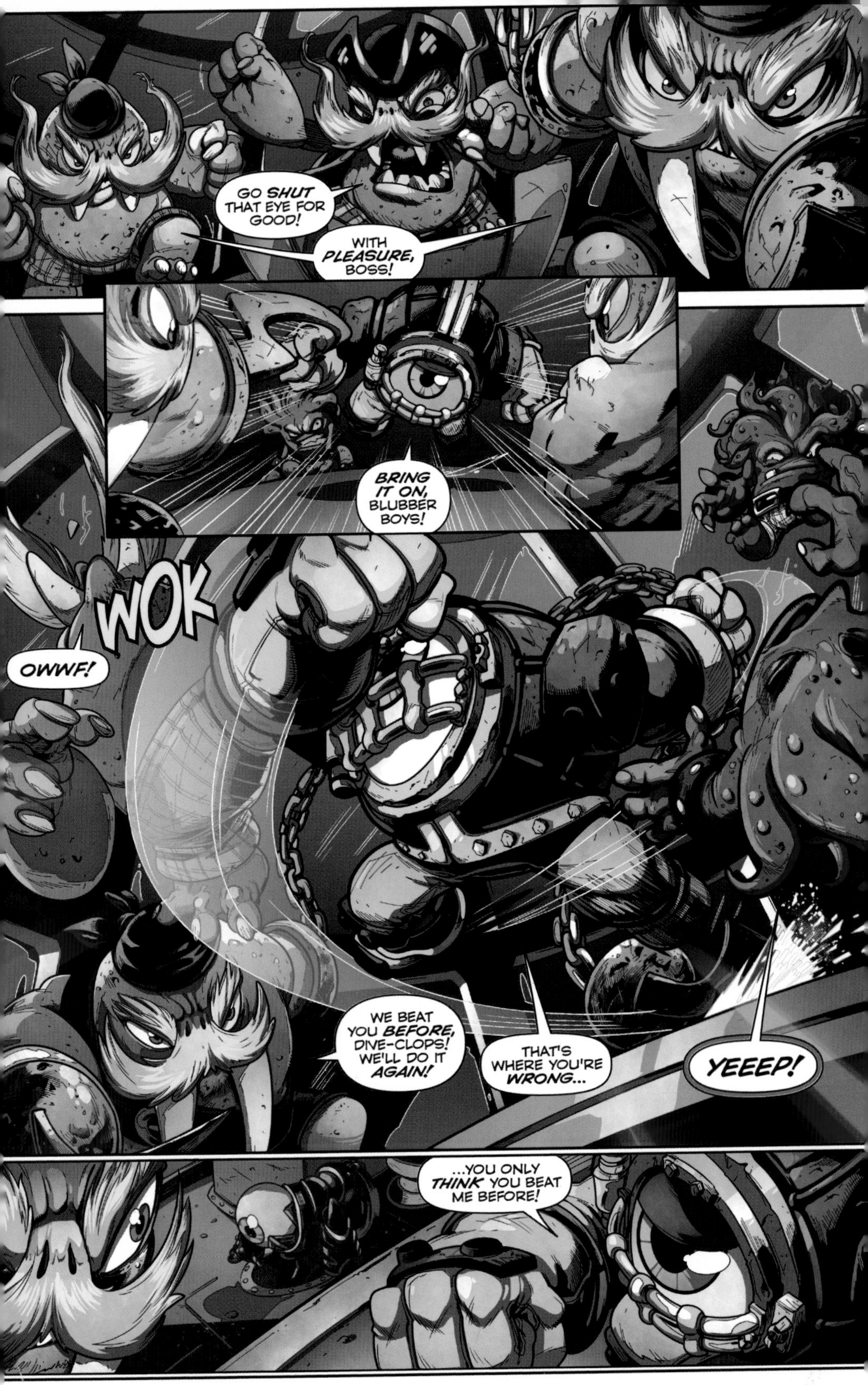
GO SHUT THAT EYE FOR GOOD!
WITH PLEASURE, BOSS!
BRING IT ON, BLUBBER BOYS!
WOK
OWWF!
WE BEAT YOU BEFORE, DIVE-CLOPS! WE'LL DO IT AGAIN!
THAT'S WHERE YOU'RE WRONG...
YEEEP!
...YOU ONLY THINK YOU BEAT ME BEFORE!

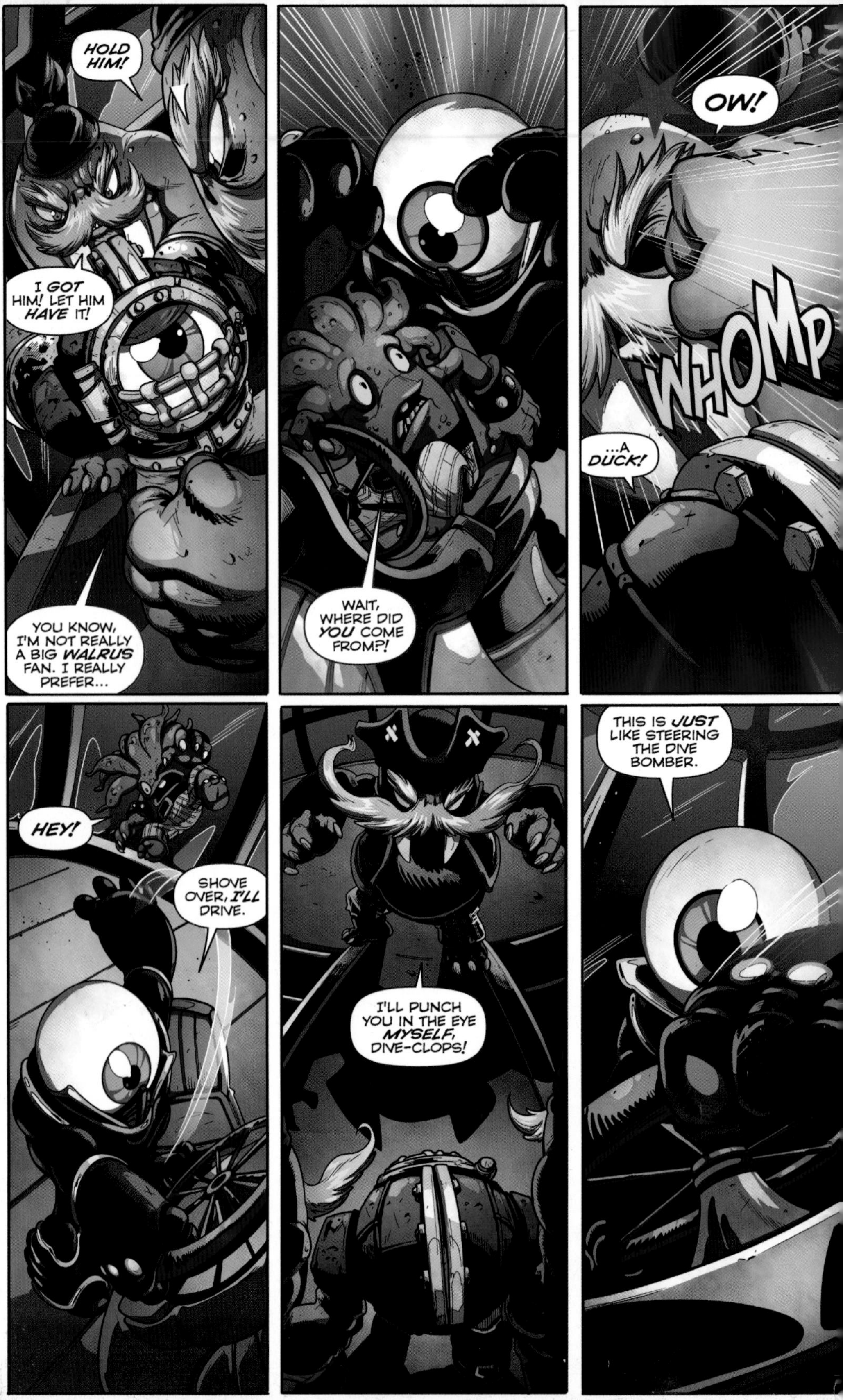
HOLD HIM!
I GOT HIM! LET HIM HAVE IT!
YOU KNOW, I'M NOT REALLY A BIG WALRUS FAN. I REALLY PREFER...
WAIT, WHERE DID YOU COME FROM?!
OW!
WHOMP
...A DUCK!
HEY!
SHOVE OVER, I'LL DRIVE.
I'LL PUNCH YOU IN THE EYE MYSELF, DIVE-CLOPS!
THIS IS JUST LIKE STEERING THE DIVE BOMBER.

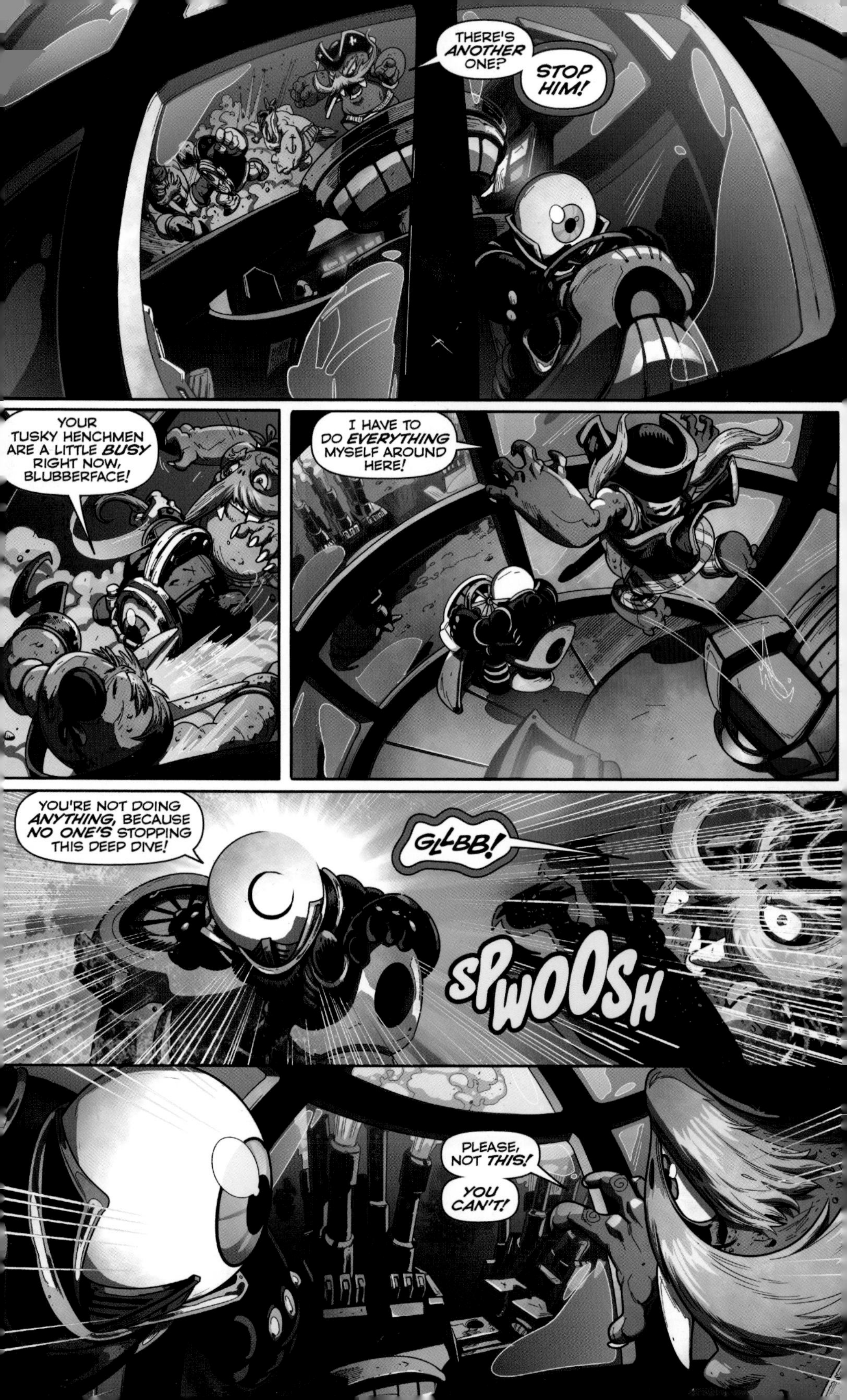
THERE'S ANOTHER ONE?
STOP HIM!
YOUR TUSKY HENCHMEN ARE A LITTLE BUSY RIGHT NOW, BLUBBERFACE!
I HAVE TO DO EVERYTHING MYSELF AROUND HERE!
YOU'RE NOT DOING ANYTHING, BECAUSE NO ONE'S STOPPING THIS DEEP DIVE!
GLLBB!
SPWOOSH
PLEASE, NOT THIS!
YOU CAN'T!

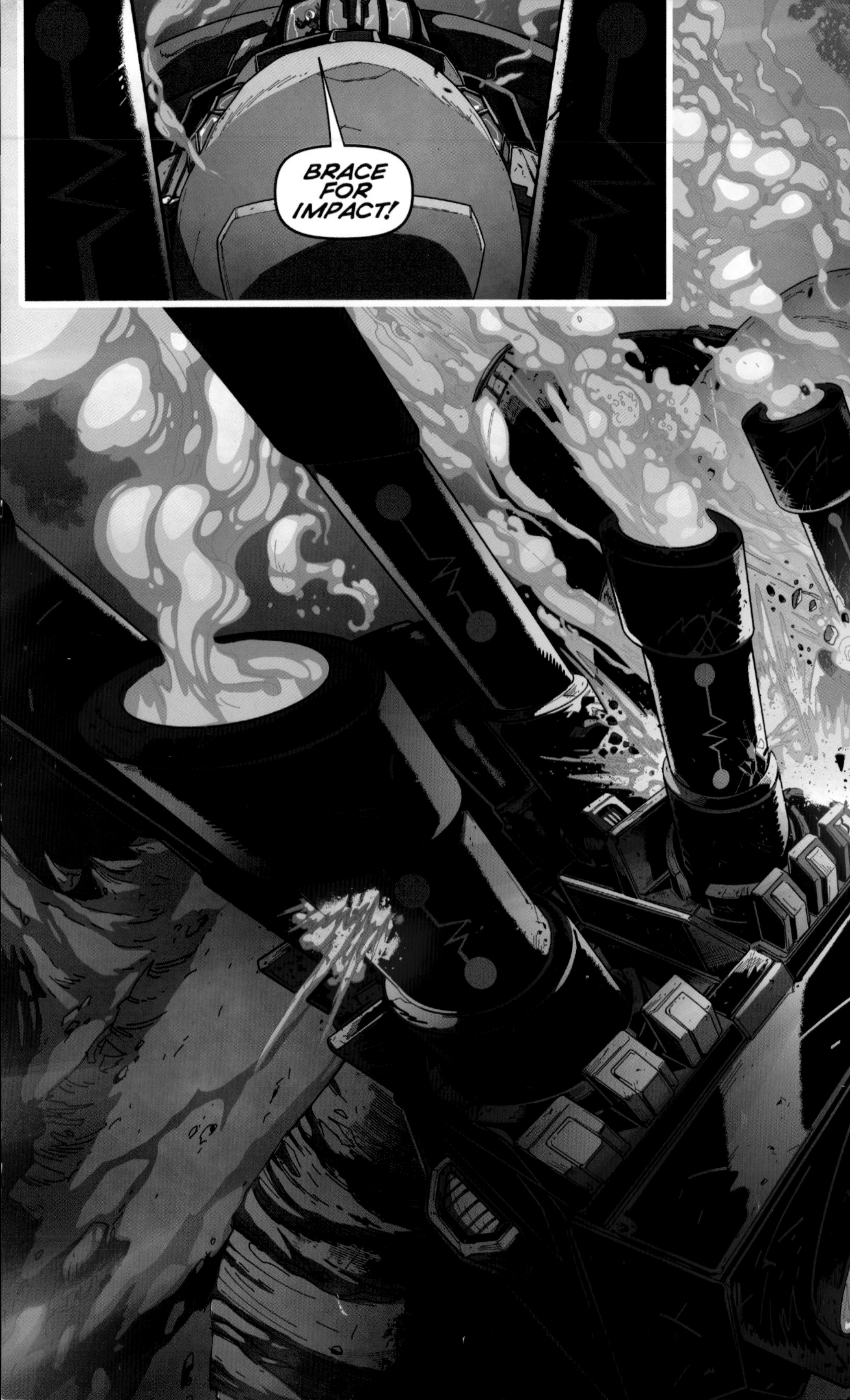
BRACE FOR IMPACT!

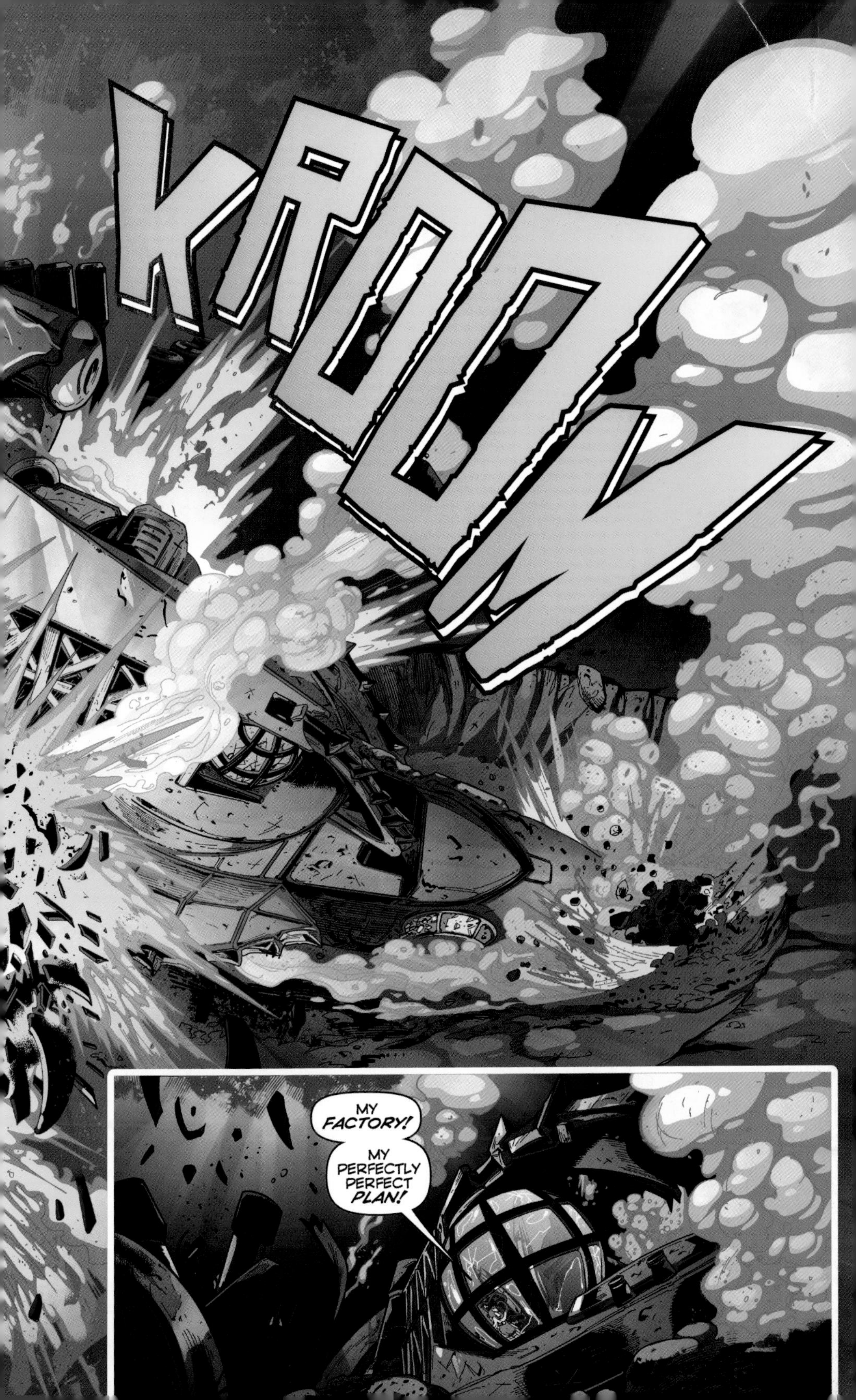
KRDOOM
MY FACTORY!
MY PERFECTLY PERFECT PLAN!

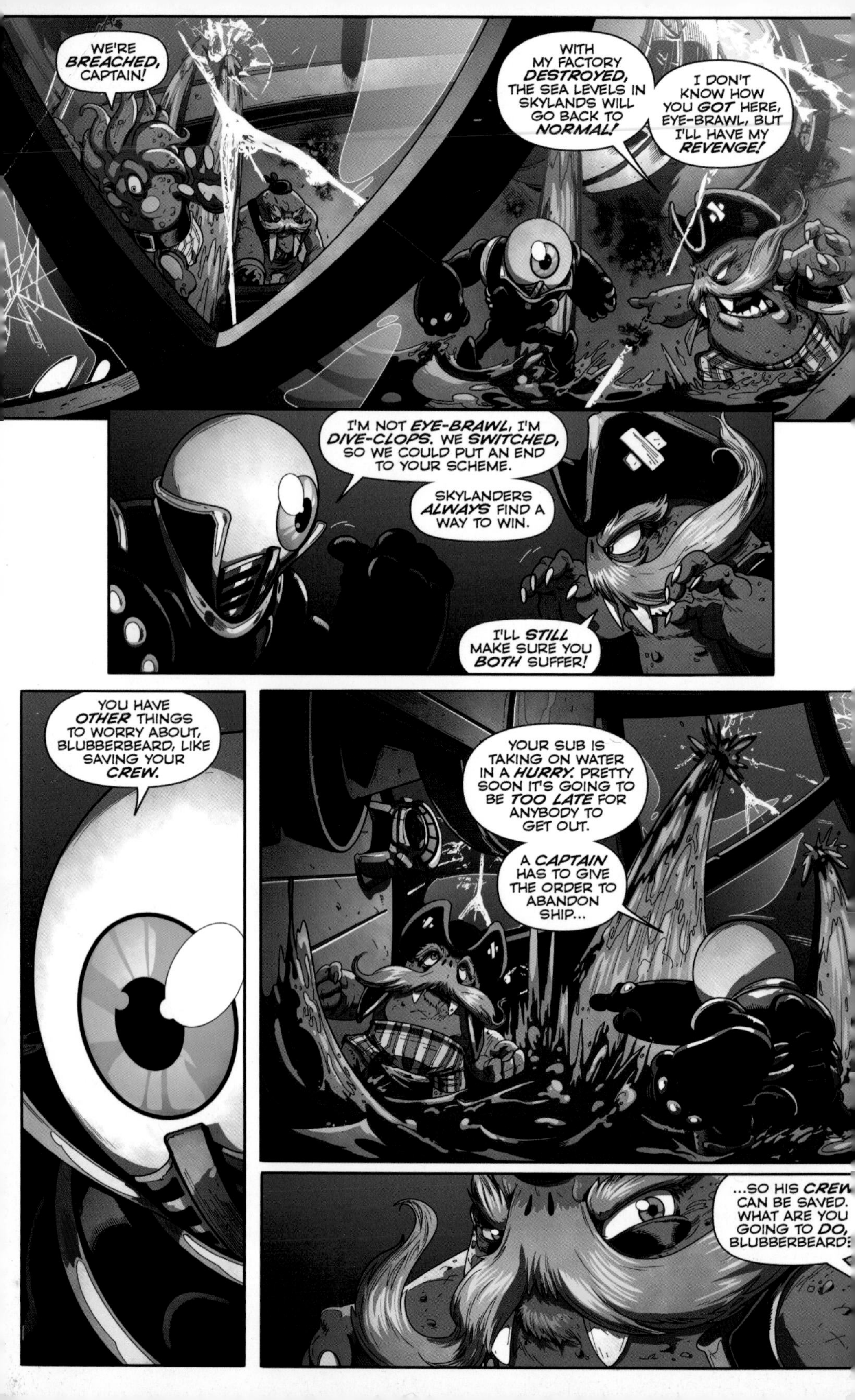
WE'RE BREACHED, CAPTAIN!
WITH MY FACTORY DESTROYED, THE SEA LEVELS IN SKYLANDS WILL GO BACK TO NORMAL!
I DON'T KNOW HOW YOU GOT HERE, EYE-BRAWL, BUT I'LL HAVE MY REVENGE!
I'M NOT EYE-BRAWL, I'M DIVE-CLOPS. WE SWITCHED, SO WE COULD PUT AN END TO YOUR SCHEME.
SKYLANDERS ALWAYS FIND A WAY TO WIN.
I'LL STILL MAKE SURE YOU BOTH SUFFER!
YOU HAVE OTHER THINGS TO WORRY ABOUT, BLUBBERBEARD, LIKE SAVING YOUR CREW.
YOUR SUB IS TAKING ON WATER IN A HURRY. PRETTY SOON IT'S GOING TO BE TOO LATE FOR ANYBODY TO GET OUT.
A CAPTAIN HAS TO GIVE THE ORDER TO ABANDON SHIP...
...SO HIS CREW CAN BE SAVED. WHAT ARE YOU GOING TO DO, BLUBBERBEARD?

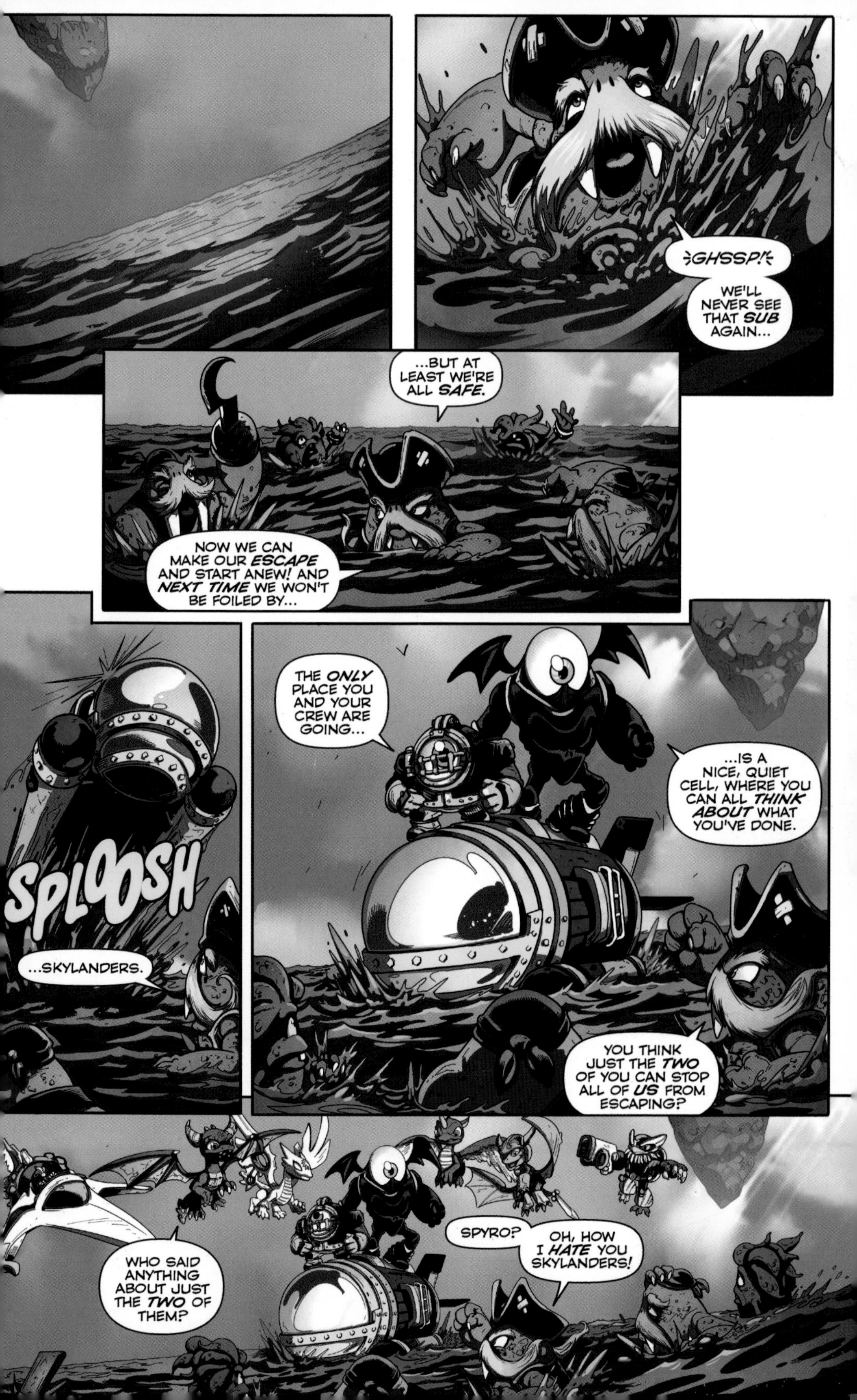
GHSSP!
WE'LL NEVER SEE THAT *SUB* AGAIN...
...BUT AT LEAST WE'RE ALL *SAFE*.
NOW WE CAN MAKE OUR *ESCAPE* AND START ANEW! AND *NEXT TIME* WE WON'T BE FOILED BY...
SPLOOSH
...SKYLANDERS.
THE *ONLY* PLACE YOU AND YOUR CREW ARE GOING...
...IS A NICE, QUIET CELL, WHERE YOU CAN ALL *THINK ABOUT* WHAT YOU'VE DONE.
YOU THINK JUST THE *TWO* OF YOU CAN STOP ALL OF *US* FROM ESCAPING?
WHO SAID ANYTHING ABOUT JUST THE *TWO* OF THEM?
SPYRO?
OH, HOW I *HATE* YOU SKYLANDERS!

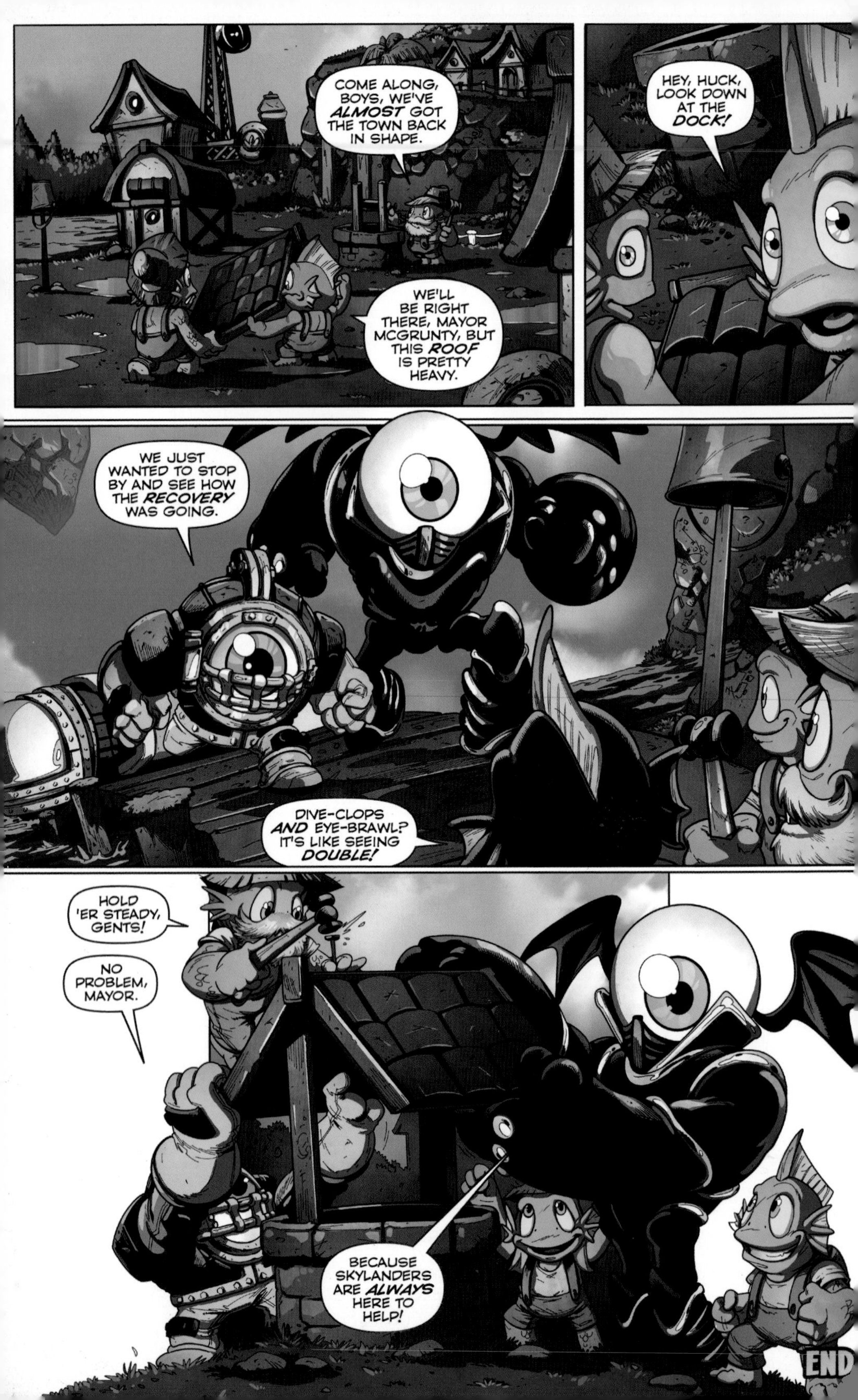

COME ALONG, BOYS, WE'VE *ALMOST* GOT THE TOWN BACK IN SHAPE.
WE'LL BE RIGHT THERE, MAYOR MCGRUNTY, BUT THIS *ROOF* IS PRETTY HEAVY.
HEY, HUCK, LOOK DOWN AT THE *DOCK!*
WE JUST WANTED TO STOP BY AND SEE HOW THE *RECOVERY* WAS GOING.
DIVE-CLOPS *AND* EYE-BRAWL? IT'S LIKE SEEING *DOUBLE!*
HOLD 'ER STEADY, GENTS!
NO PROBLEM, MAYOR.
BECAUSE SKYLANDERS ARE *ALWAYS* HERE TO HELP!
END

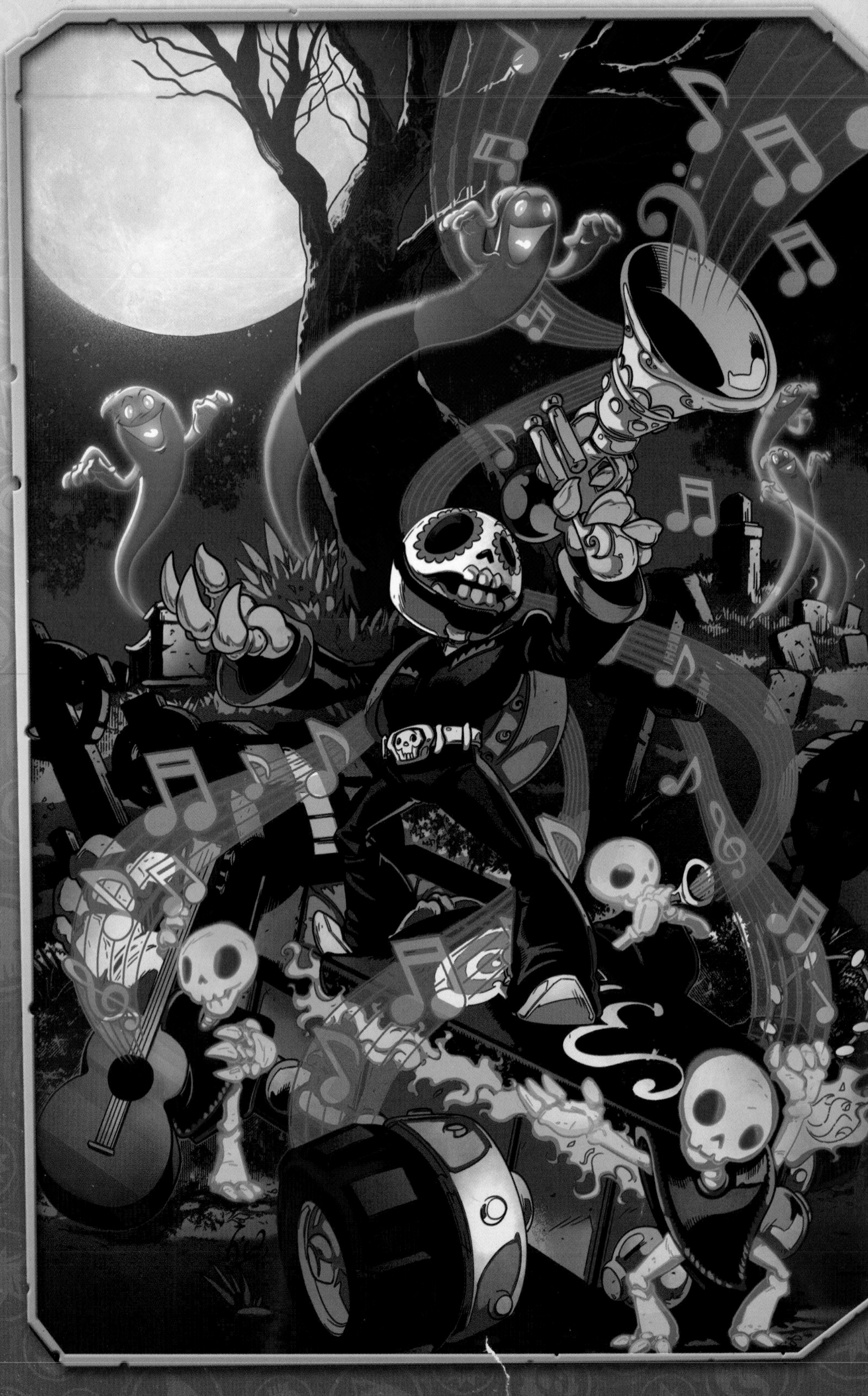

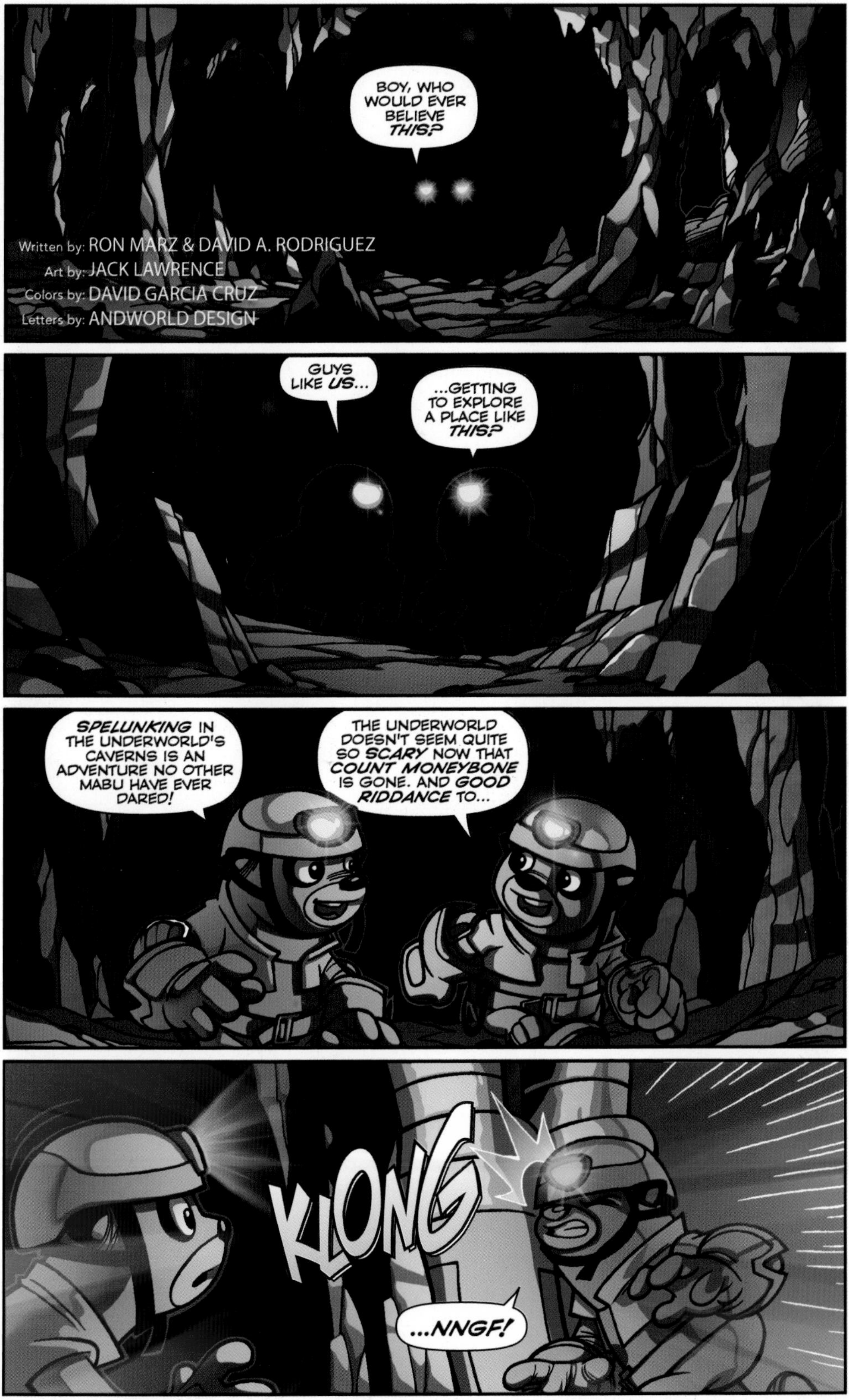
BOY, WHO WOULD EVER BELIEVE THIS?
Written by: RON MARZ & DAVID A. RODRIGUEZ
Art by: JACK LAWRENCE
Colors by: DAVID GARCIA CRUZ
Letters by: ANDWORLD DESIGN
GUYS LIKE US...
...GETTING TO EXPLORE A PLACE LIKE THIS?
SPELUNKING IN THE UNDERWORLD'S CAVERNS IS AN ADVENTURE NO OTHER MABU HAVE EVER DARED!
THE UNDERWORLD DOESN'T SEEM QUITE SO SCARY NOW THAT COUNT MONEYBONE IS GONE. AND GOOD RIDDANCE TO...
KLONG
...NNGF!

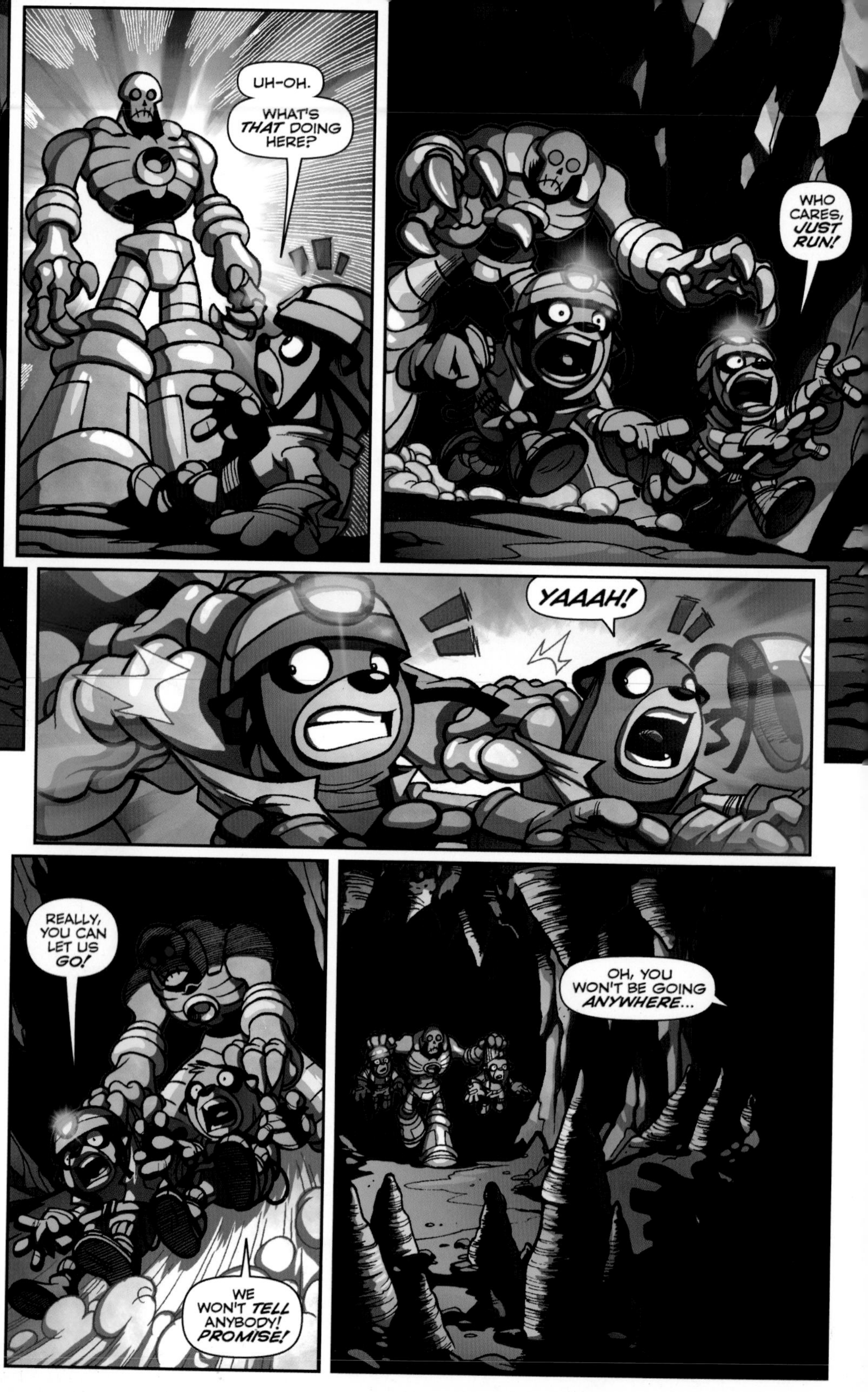
UH-OH.
WHAT'S *THAT* DOING HERE?
WHO CARES, *JUST RUN!*
YAAAH!
REALLY, YOU CAN LET US *GO!*
WE WON'T *TELL* ANYBODY! *PROMISE!*
OH, YOU WON'T BE GOING *ANYWHERE*...

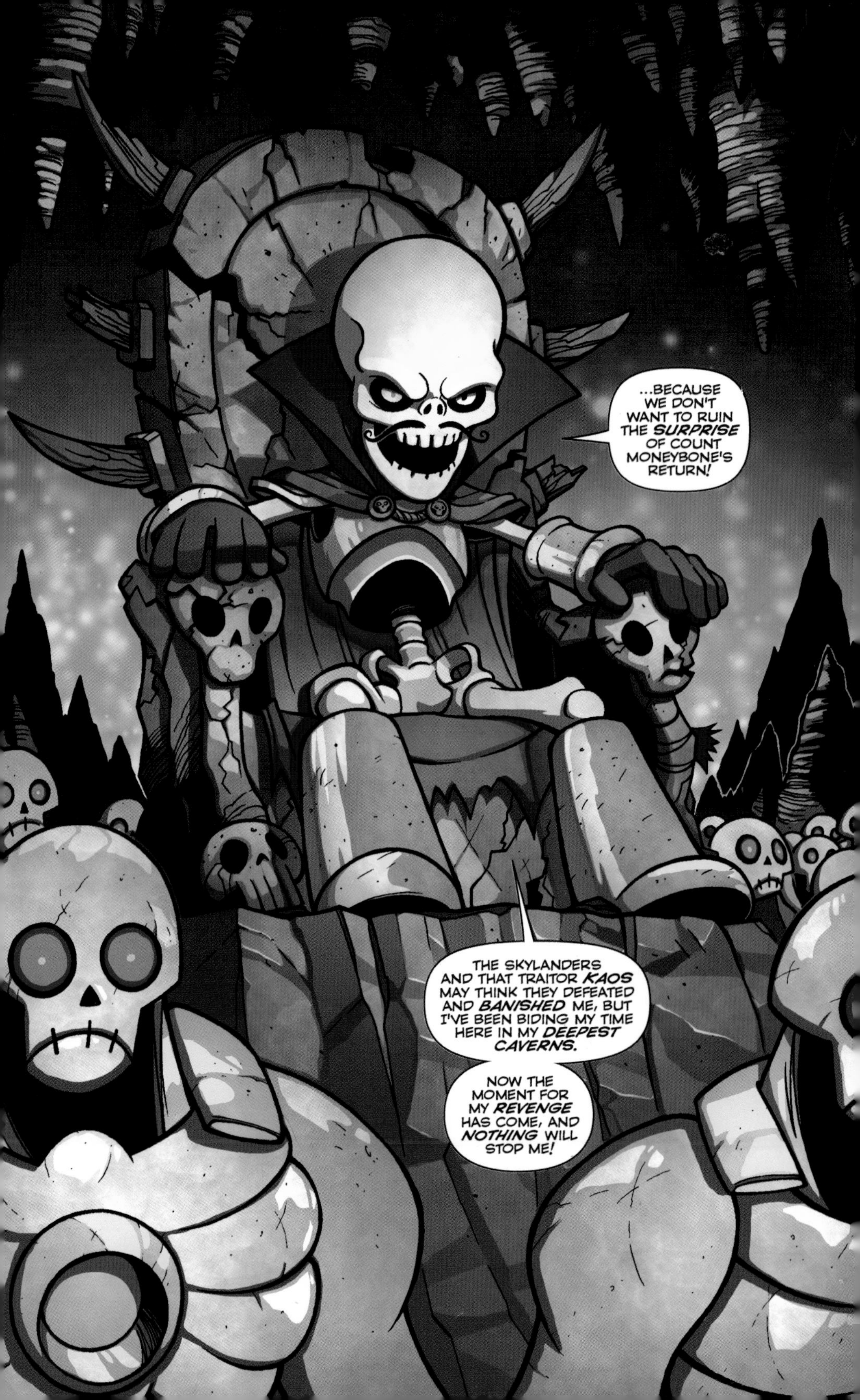
...BECAUSE WE DON'T WANT TO RUIN THE *SURPRISE* OF COUNT MONEYBONE'S RETURN!
THE SKYLANDERS AND THAT TRAITOR *KAOS* MAY THINK THEY DEFEATED AND *BANISHED* ME, BUT I'VE BEEN BIDING MY TIME HERE IN MY *DEEPEST CAVERNS.*
NOW THE MOMENT FOR MY *REVENGE* HAS COME, AND *NOTHING* WILL STOP ME!

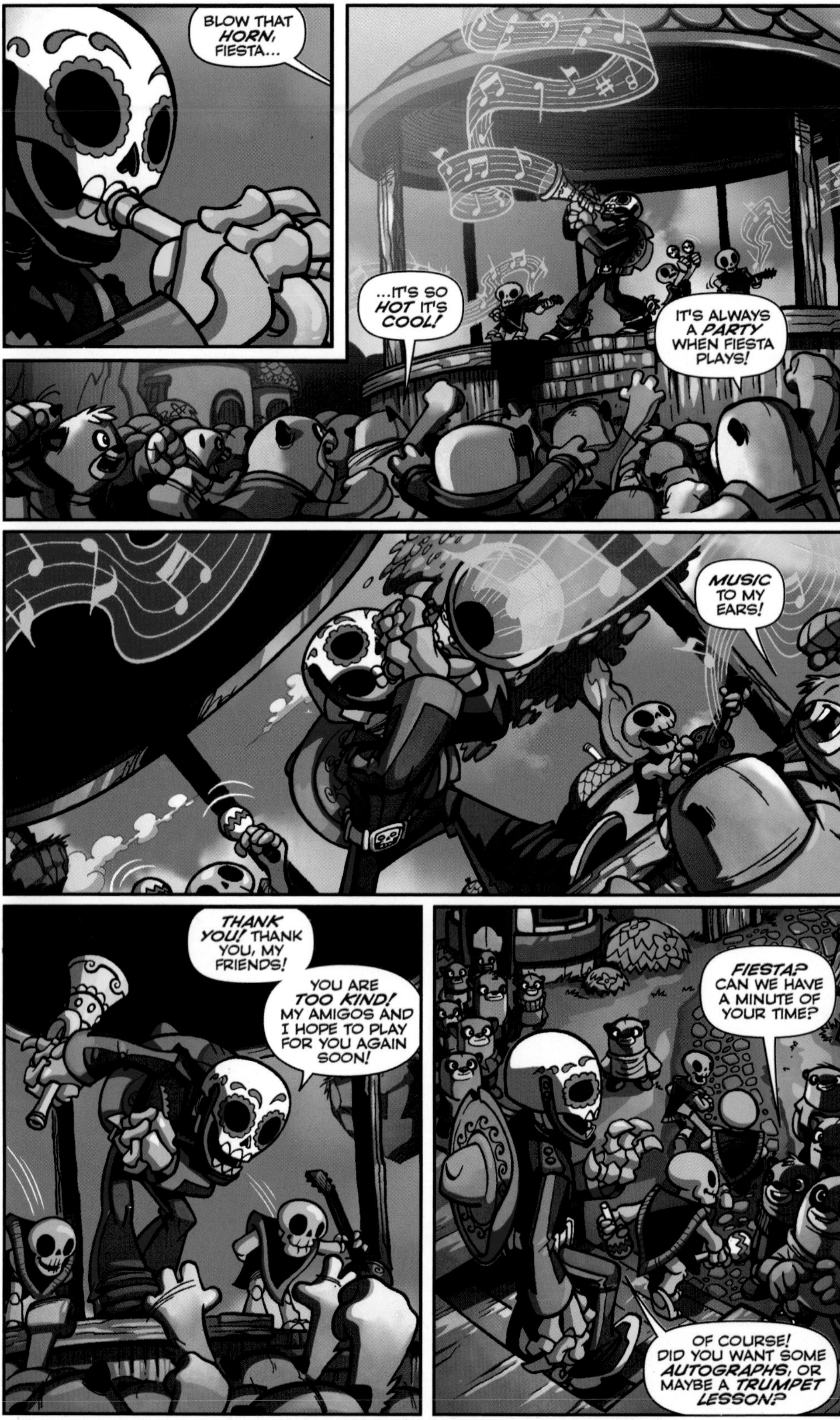
BLOW THAT HORN, FIESTA...
...IT'S SO HOT IT'S COOL!
IT'S ALWAYS A PARTY WHEN FIESTA PLAYS!
MUSIC TO MY EARS!
THANK YOU! THANK YOU, MY FRIENDS!
YOU ARE TOO KIND! MY AMIGOS AND I HOPE TO PLAY FOR YOU AGAIN SOON!
FIESTA? CAN WE HAVE A MINUTE OF YOUR TIME?
OF COURSE! DID YOU WANT SOME AUTOGRAPHS, OR MAYBE A TRUMPET LESSON?

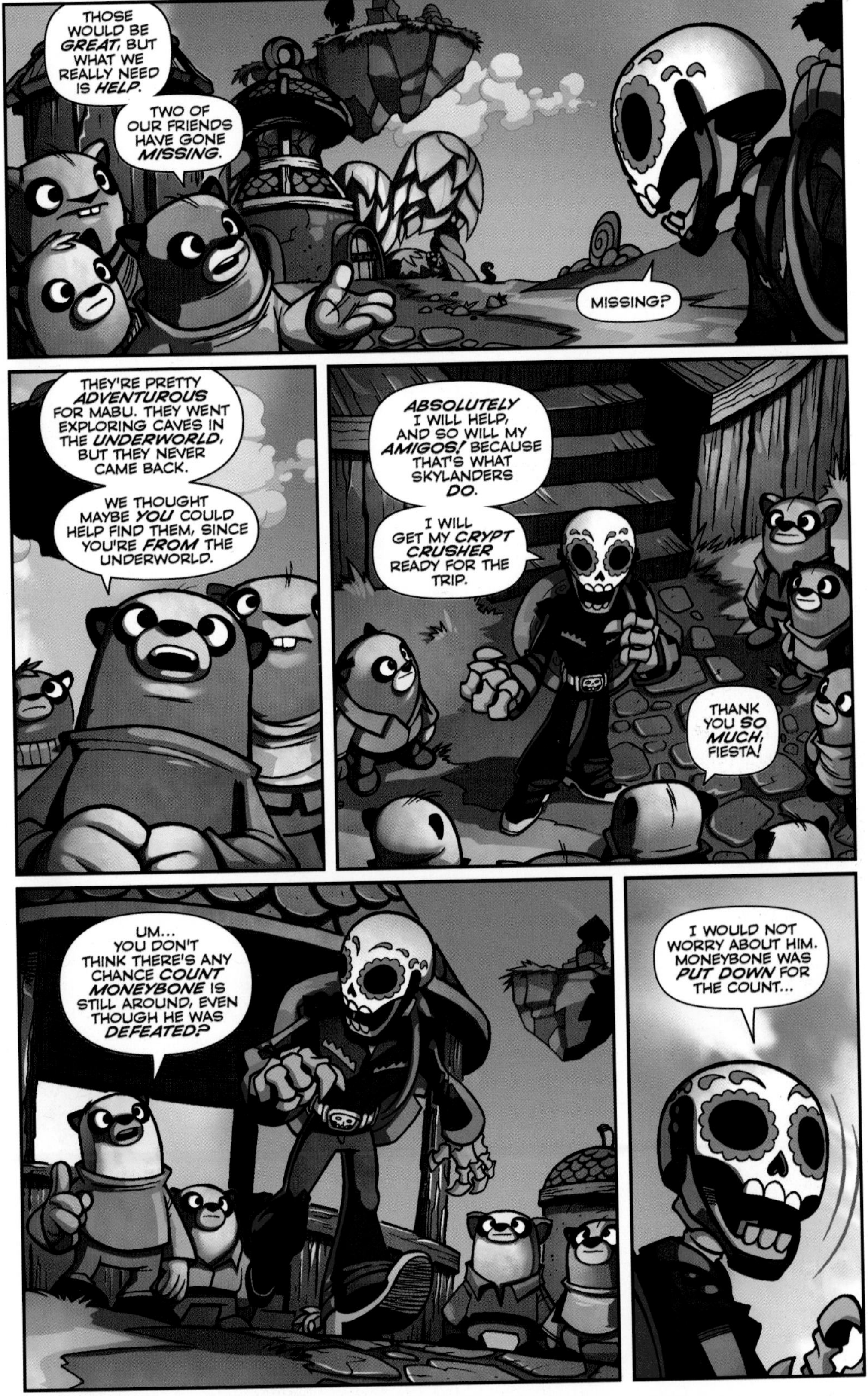
THOSE WOULD BE *GREAT,* BUT WHAT WE REALLY NEED IS *HELP*.
TWO OF OUR FRIENDS HAVE GONE *MISSING*.
MISSING?
THEY'RE PRETTY *ADVENTUROUS* FOR MABU. THEY WENT EXPLORING CAVES IN THE *UNDERWORLD*, BUT THEY NEVER CAME BACK.
WE THOUGHT MAYBE *YOU* COULD HELP FIND THEM, SINCE YOU'RE *FROM* THE UNDERWORLD.
ABSOLUTELY I WILL HELP, AND SO WILL MY *AMIGOS!* BECAUSE THAT'S WHAT SKYLANDERS *DO*.
I WILL GET MY *CRYPT CRUSHER* READY FOR THE TRIP.
THANK YOU *SO MUCH*, FIESTA!
UM... YOU DON'T THINK THERE'S ANY CHANCE *COUNT MONEYBONE* IS STILL AROUND, EVEN THOUGH HE WAS *DEFEATED?*
I WOULD NOT WORRY ABOUT HIM. MONEYBONE WAS *PUT DOWN* FOR THE COUNT...

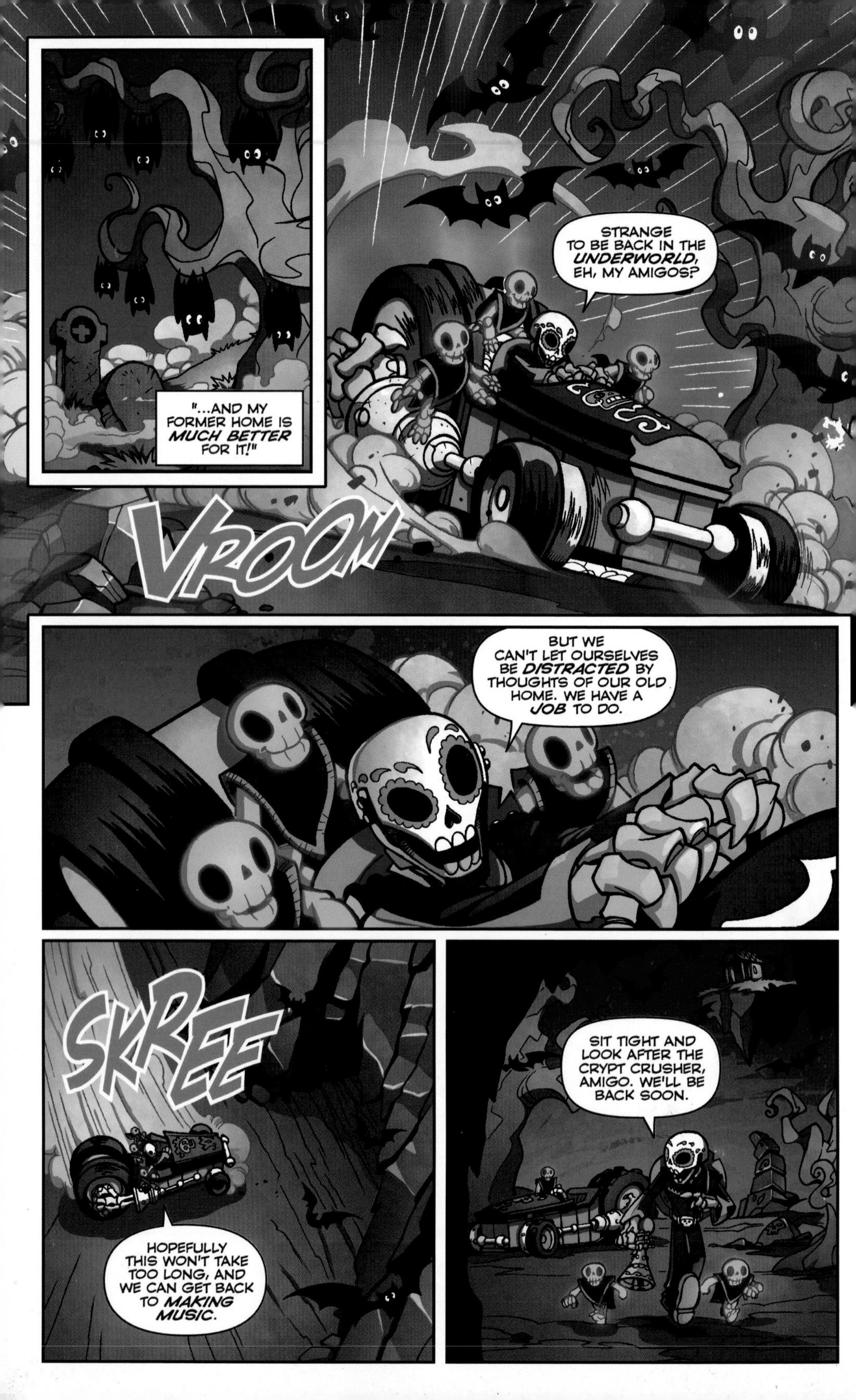
"...AND MY FORMER HOME IS MUCH BETTER FOR IT!"
STRANGE TO BE BACK IN THE UNDERWORLD, EH, MY AMIGOS?
VROOM
BUT WE CAN'T LET OURSELVES BE DISTRACTED BY THOUGHTS OF OUR OLD HOME. WE HAVE A JOB TO DO.
SKREE
HOPEFULLY THIS WON'T TAKE TOO LONG, AND WE CAN GET BACK TO MAKING MUSIC.
SIT TIGHT AND LOOK AFTER THE CRYPT CRUSHER, AMIGO. WE'LL BE BACK SOON.

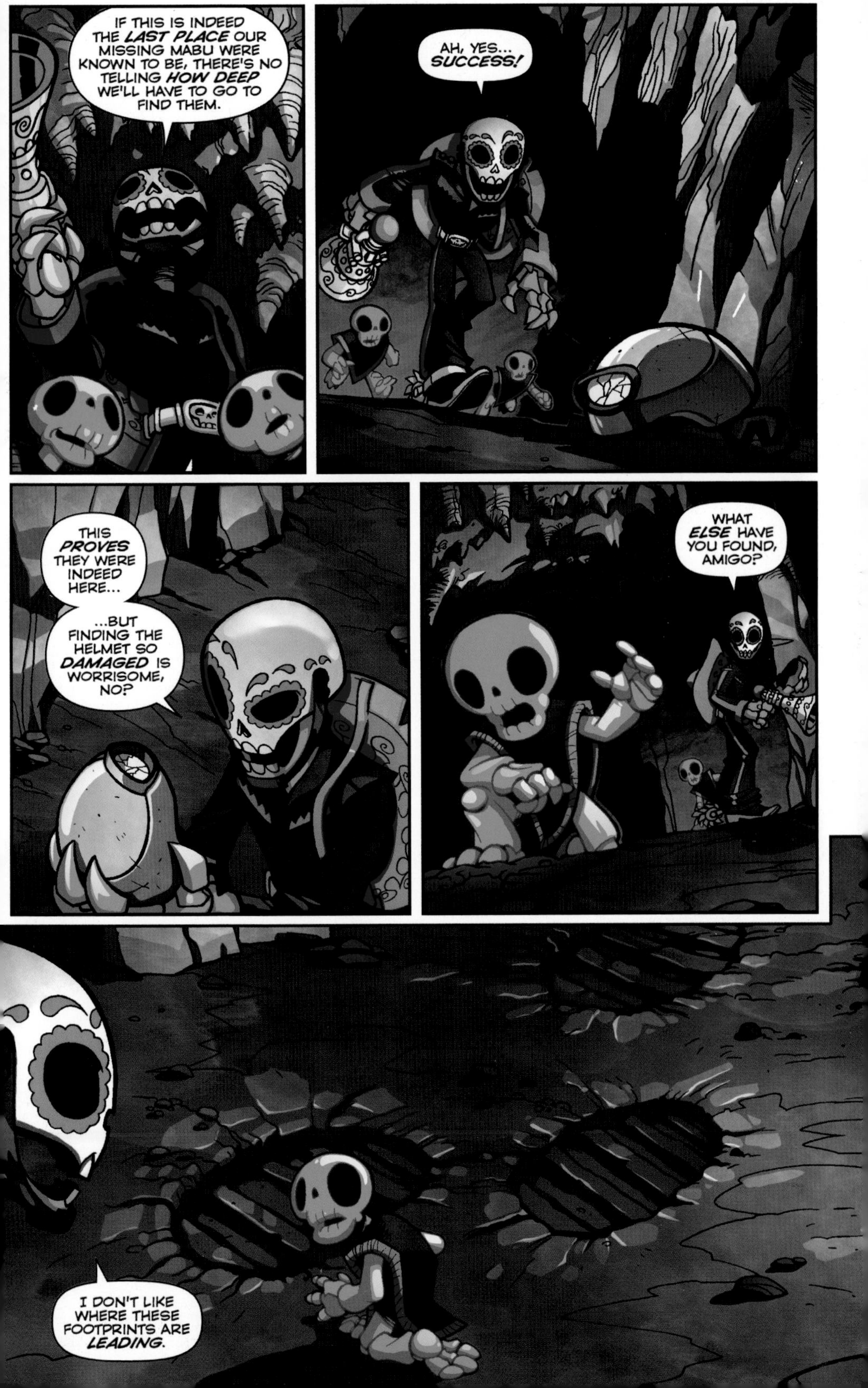
IF THIS IS INDEED THE LAST PLACE OUR MISSING MABU WERE KNOWN TO BE, THERE'S NO TELLING HOW DEEP WE'LL HAVE TO GO TO FIND THEM.
AH, YES... SUCCESS!
THIS PROVES THEY WERE INDEED HERE...
...BUT FINDING THE HELMET SO DAMAGED IS WORRISOME, NO?
WHAT ELSE HAVE YOU FOUND, AMIGO?
I DON'T LIKE WHERE THESE FOOTPRINTS ARE LEADING.

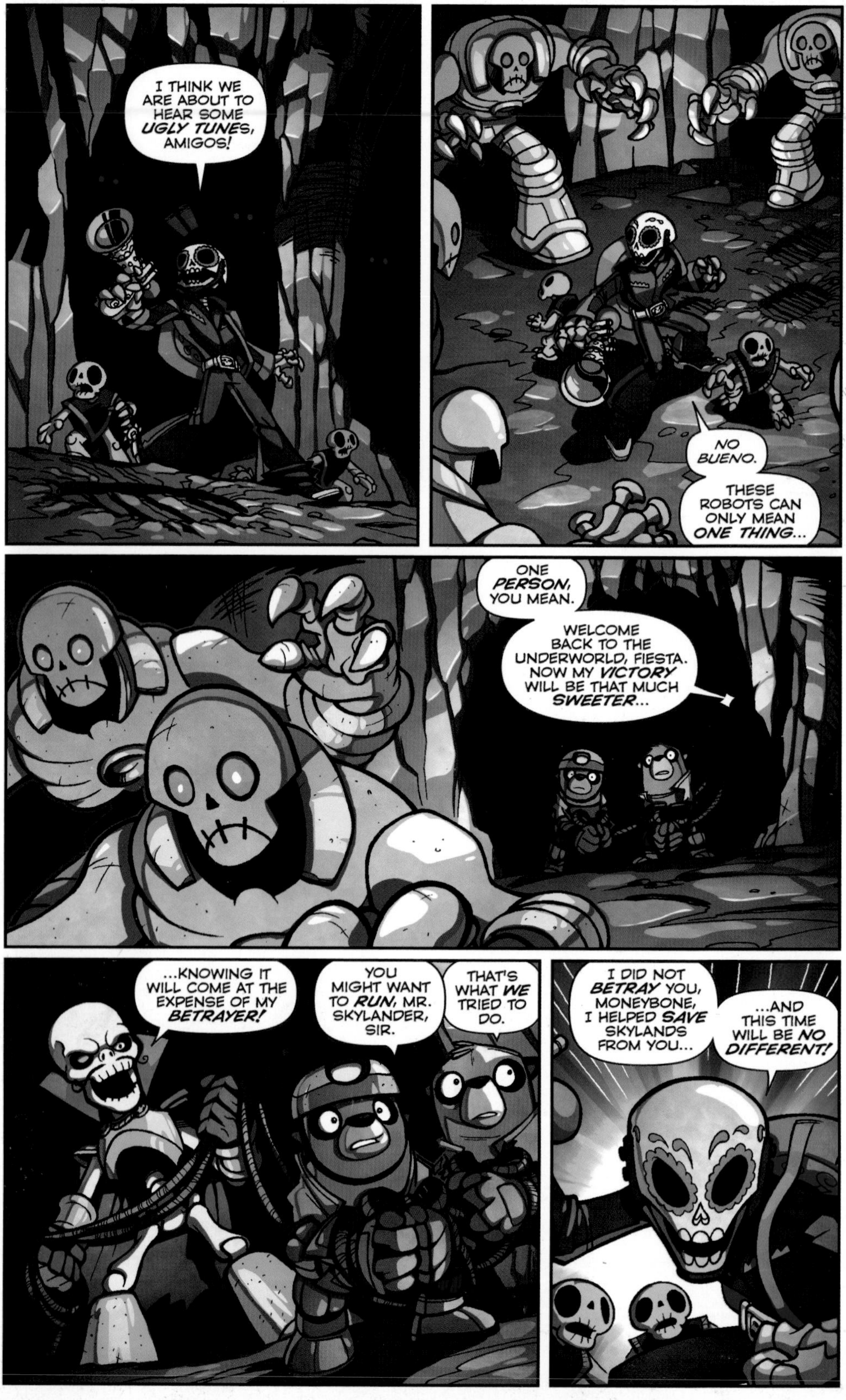
I THINK WE ARE ABOUT TO HEAR SOME UGLY TUNES, AMIGOS!
NO BUENO.
THESE ROBOTS CAN ONLY MEAN ONE THING...
ONE PERSON, YOU MEAN.
WELCOME BACK TO THE UNDERWORLD, FIESTA. NOW MY VICTORY WILL BE THAT MUCH SWEETER...
...KNOWING IT WILL COME AT THE EXPENSE OF MY BETRAYER!
YOU MIGHT WANT TO RUN, MR. SKYLANDER, SIR.
THAT'S WHAT WE TRIED TO DO.
I DID NOT BETRAY YOU, MONEYBONE, I HELPED SAVE SKYLANDS FROM YOU...
...AND THIS TIME WILL BE NO DIFFERENT!

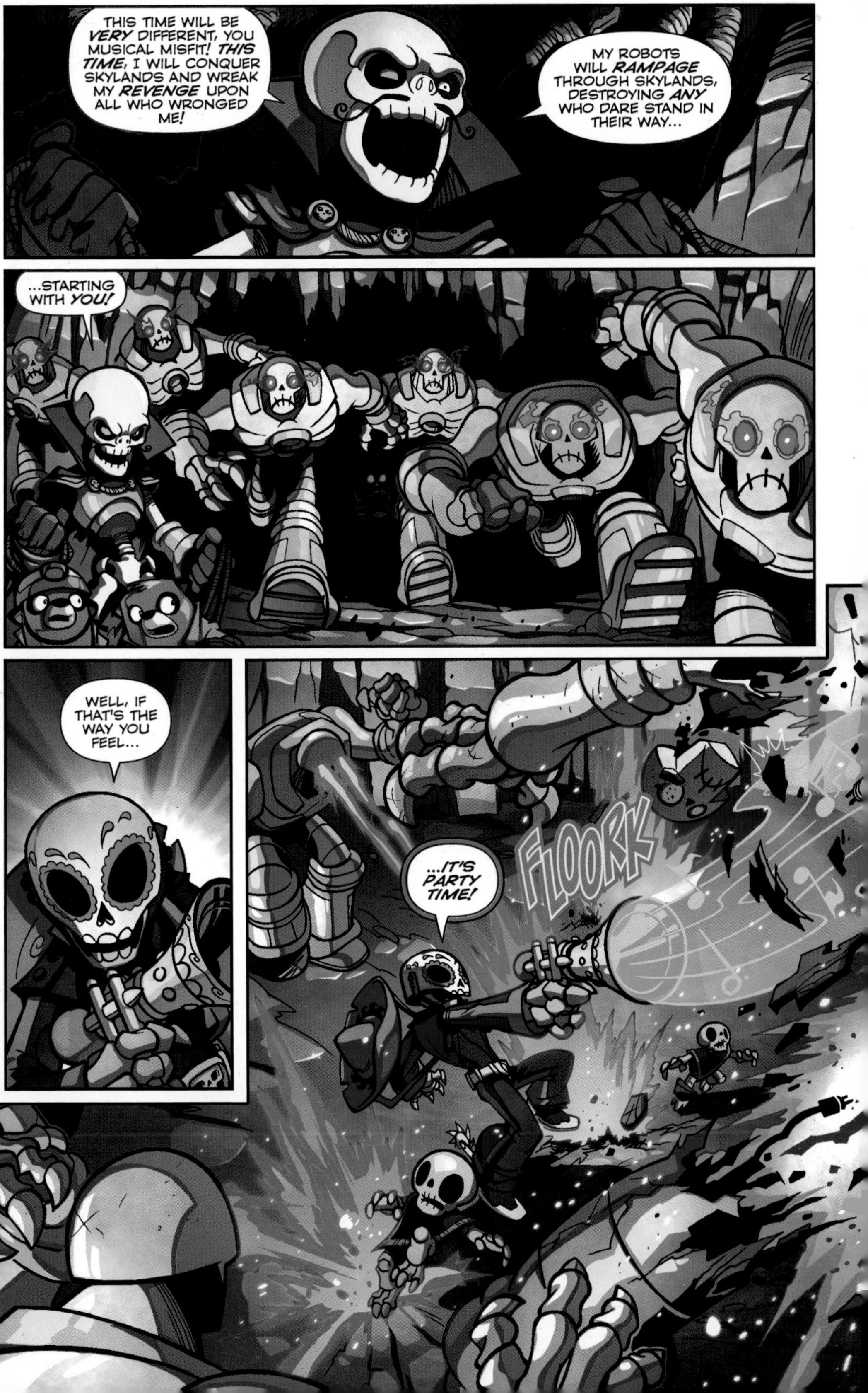
THIS TIME WILL BE VERY DIFFERENT, YOU MUSICAL MISFIT! THIS TIME, I WILL CONQUER SKYLANDS AND WREAK MY REVENGE UPON ALL WHO WRONGED ME!
MY ROBOTS WILL RAMPAGE THROUGH SKYLANDS, DESTROYING ANY WHO DARE STAND IN THEIR WAY...
...STARTING WITH YOU!
WELL, IF THAT'S THE WAY YOU FEEL...
...IT'S PARTY TIME!
FLOORK

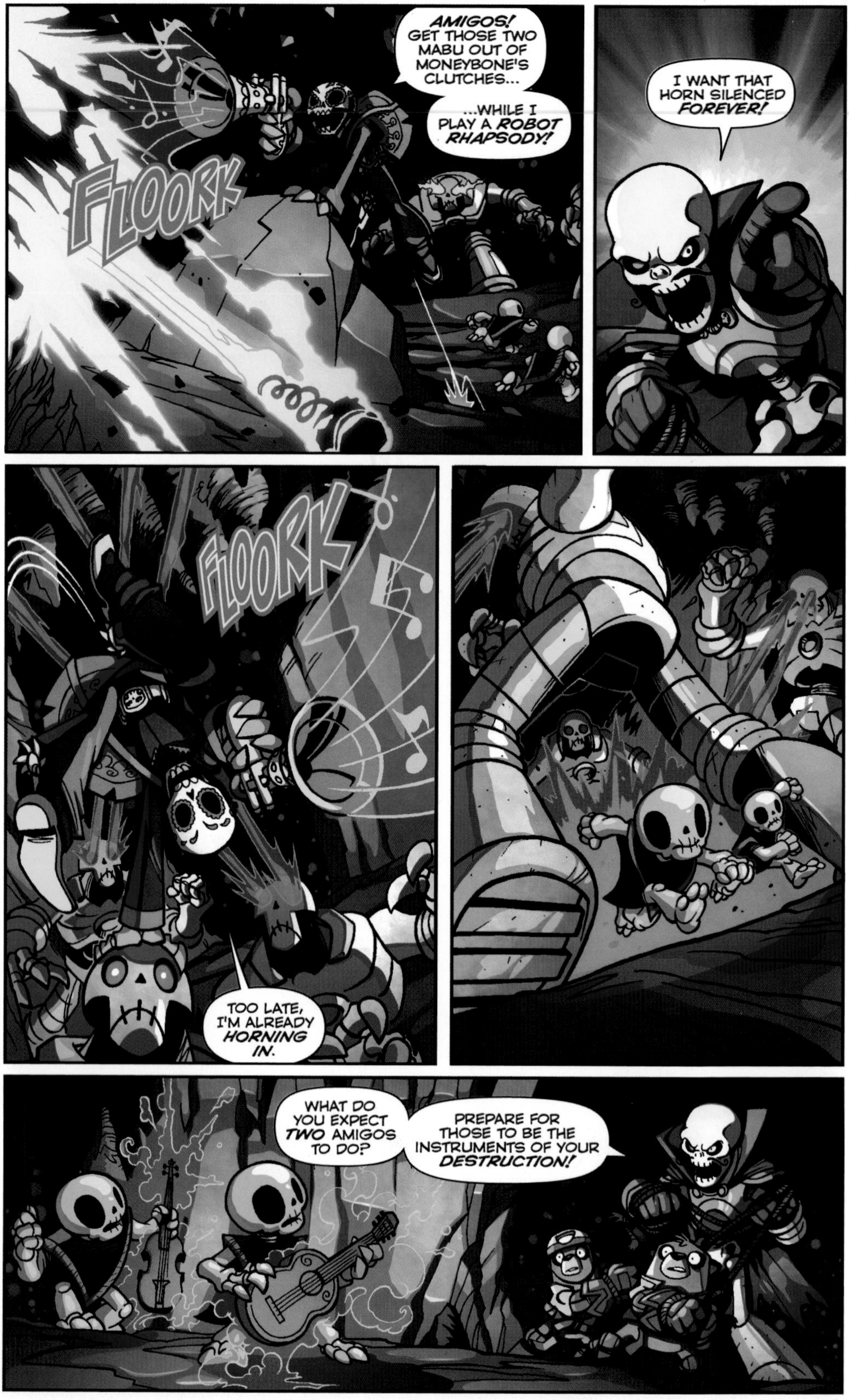
AMIGOS! GET THOSE TWO MABU OUT OF MONEYBONE'S CLUTCHES...
...WHILE I PLAY A ROBOT RHAPSODY!
FLOORK
I WANT THAT HORN SILENCED FOREVER!
FLOORK
TOO LATE, I'M ALREADY HORNING IN.
WHAT DO YOU EXPECT TWO AMIGOS TO DO?
PREPARE FOR THOSE TO BE THE INSTRUMENTS OF YOUR DESTRUCTION!

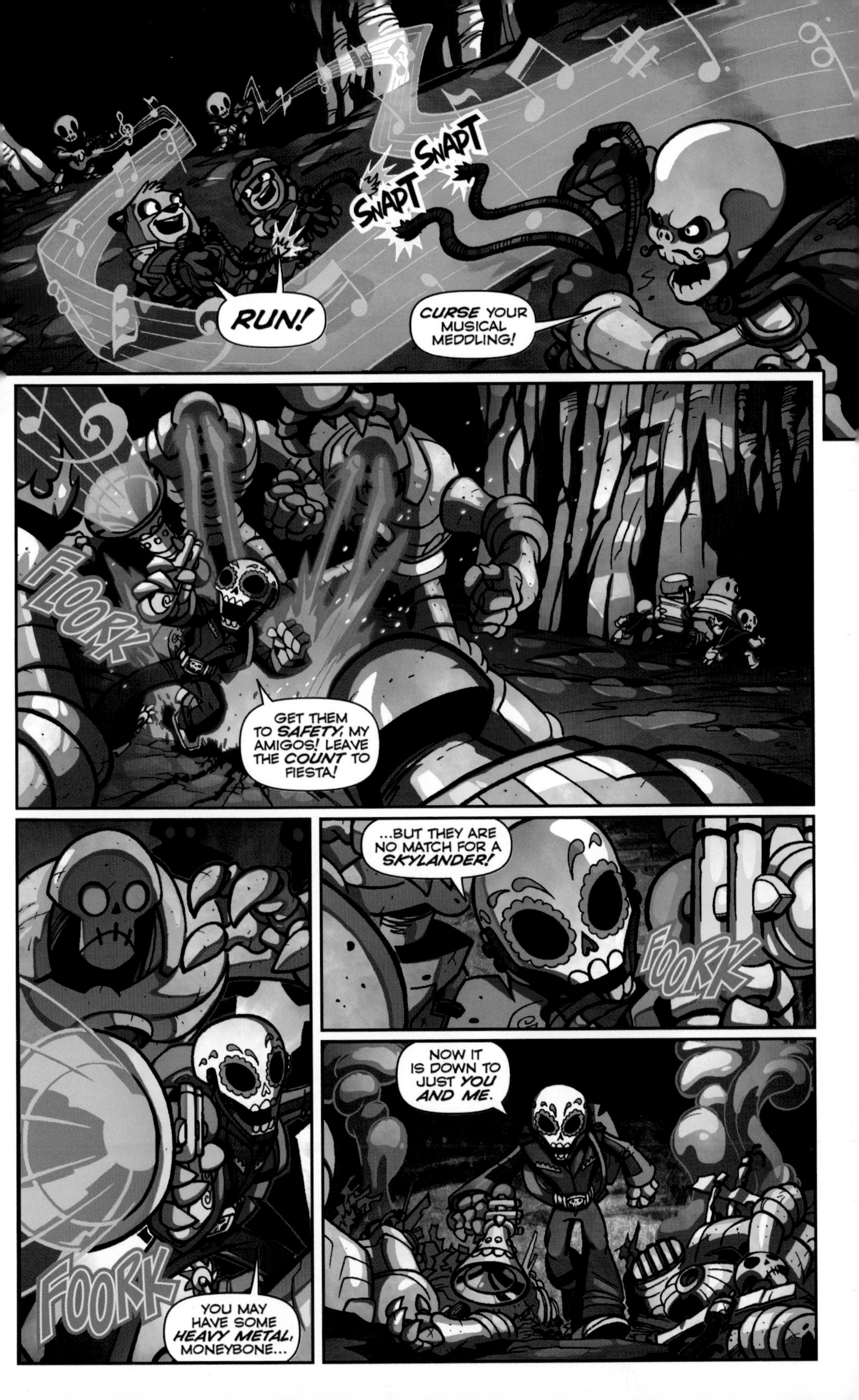
SNAPT
SNAPT
RUN!
CURSE YOUR MUSICAL MEDDLING!
FLOORK
GET THEM TO SAFETY, MY AMIGOS! LEAVE THE COUNT TO FIESTA!
FOORK
YOU MAY HAVE SOME HEAVY METAL, MONEYBONE...
...BUT THEY ARE NO MATCH FOR A SKYLANDER!
FOORK
NOW IT IS DOWN TO JUST YOU AND ME.

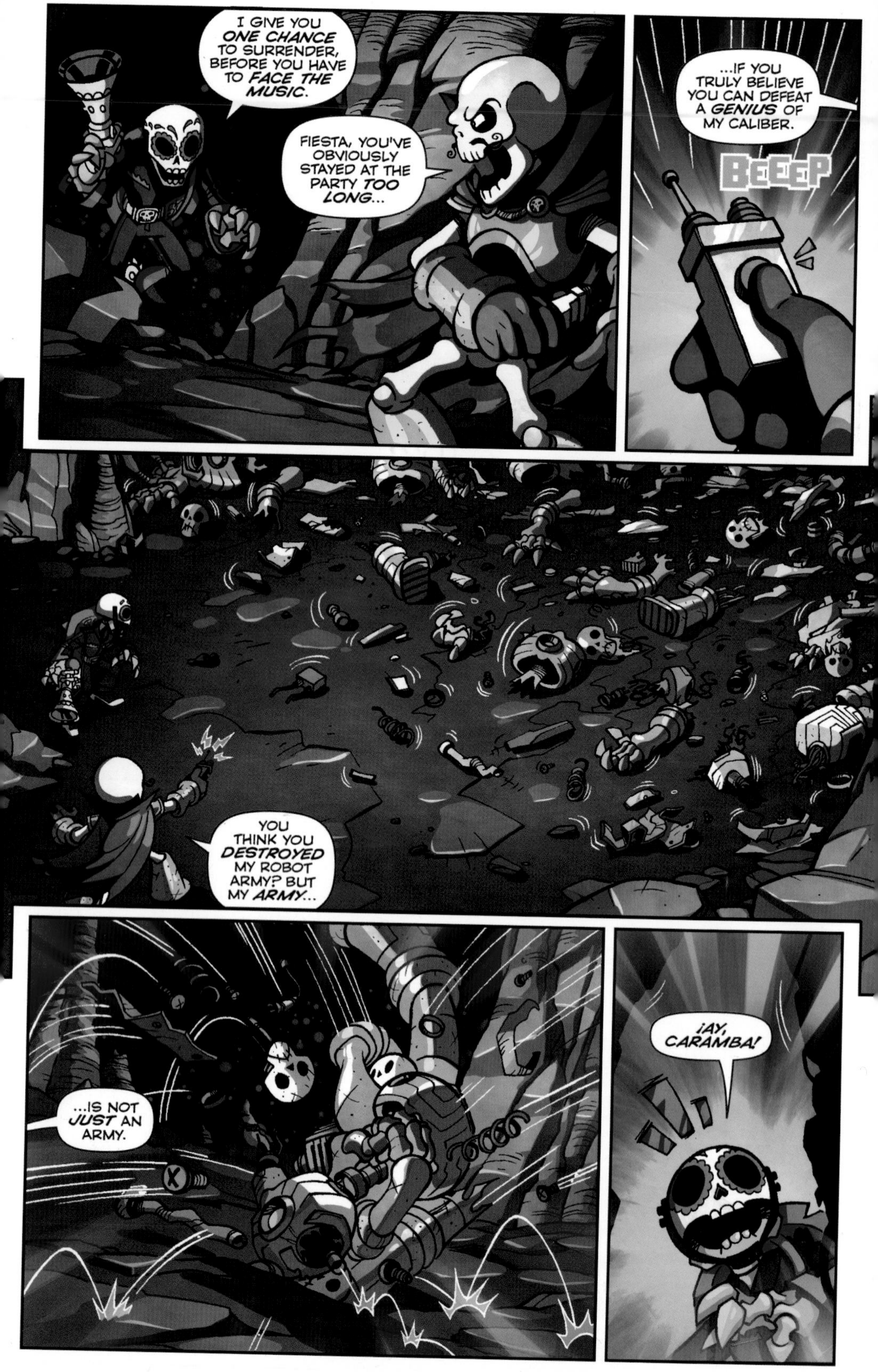
I GIVE YOU ONE CHANCE TO SURRENDER, BEFORE YOU HAVE TO FACE THE MUSIC.
FIESTA, YOU'VE OBVIOUSLY STAYED AT THE PARTY TOO LONG...
...IF YOU TRULY BELIEVE YOU CAN DEFEAT A GENIUS OF MY CALIBER.
BEEEP
YOU THINK YOU DESTROYED MY ROBOT ARMY? BUT MY ARMY...
...IS NOT JUST AN ARMY.
¡AY, CARAMBA!

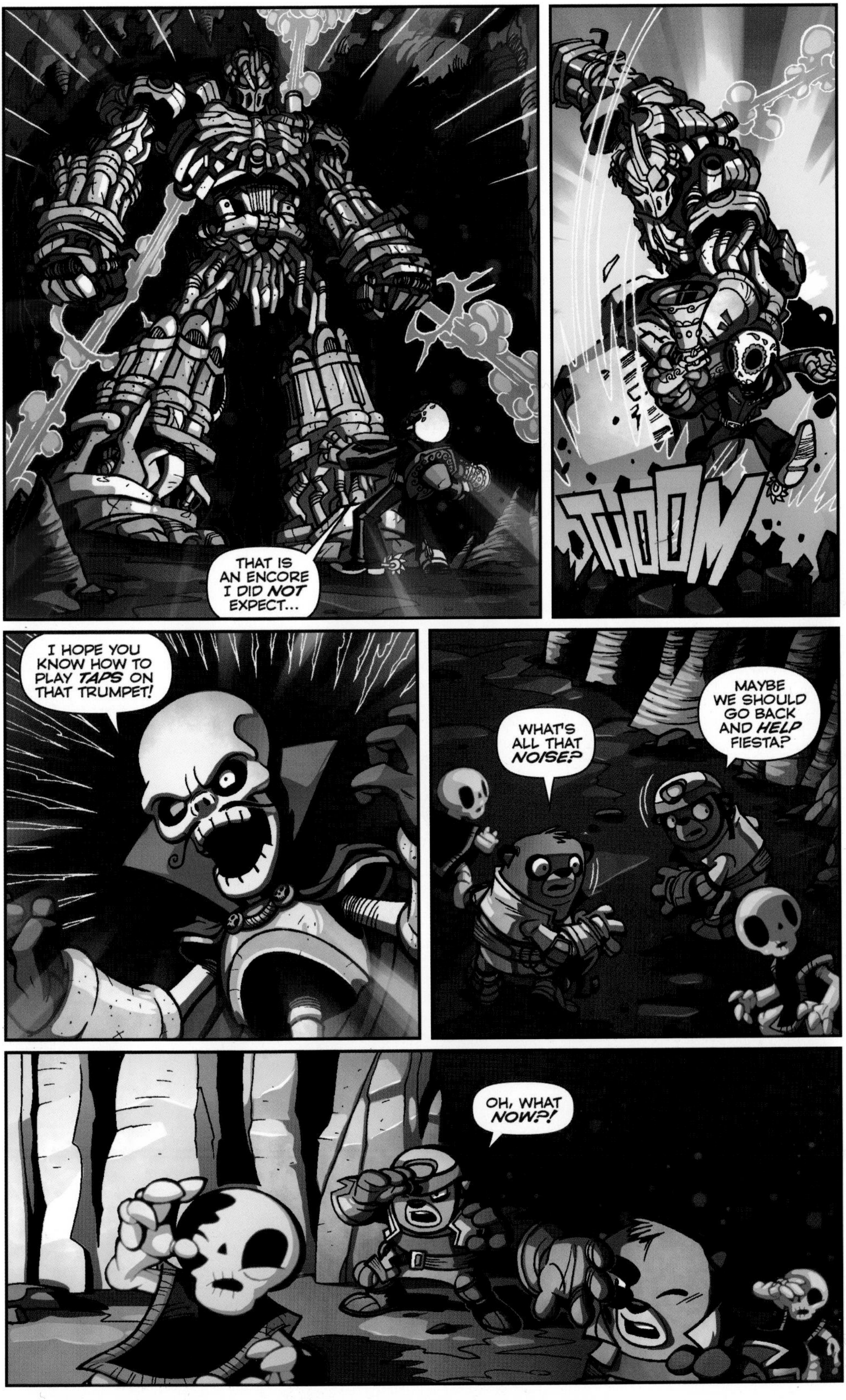
THAT IS AN ENCORE I DID *NOT* EXPECT...
THOOM
I HOPE YOU KNOW HOW TO PLAY *TAPS* ON THAT TRUMPET!
WHAT'S ALL THAT *NOISE?*
MAYBE WE SHOULD GO BACK AND *HELP* FIESTA?
OH, WHAT *NOW?!*

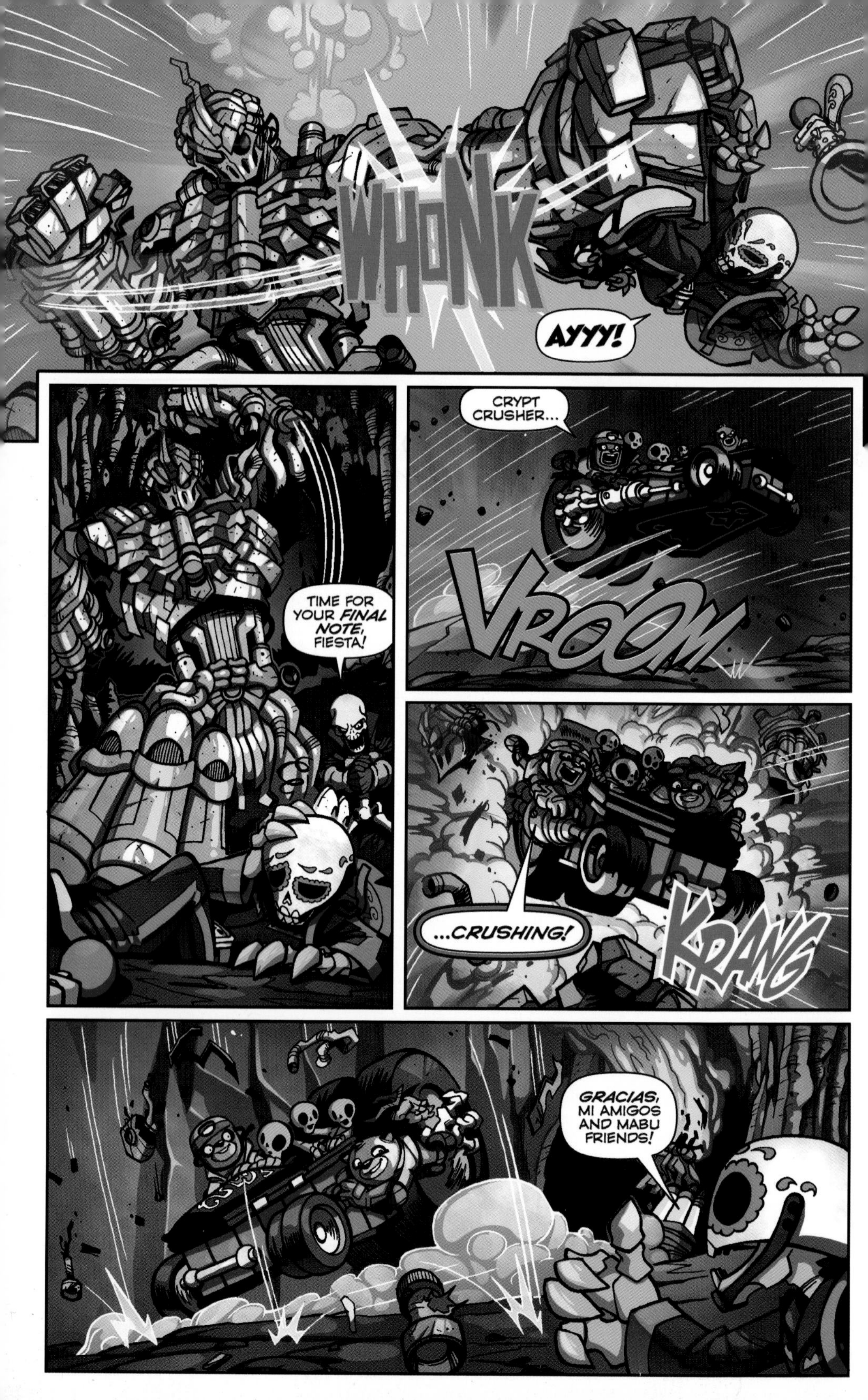
WHONK
AYYY!
TIME FOR YOUR FINAL NOTE, FIESTA!
CRYPT CRUSHER...
VROOM
...CRUSHING!
KRANG
GRACIAS, MI AMIGOS AND MABU FRIENDS!

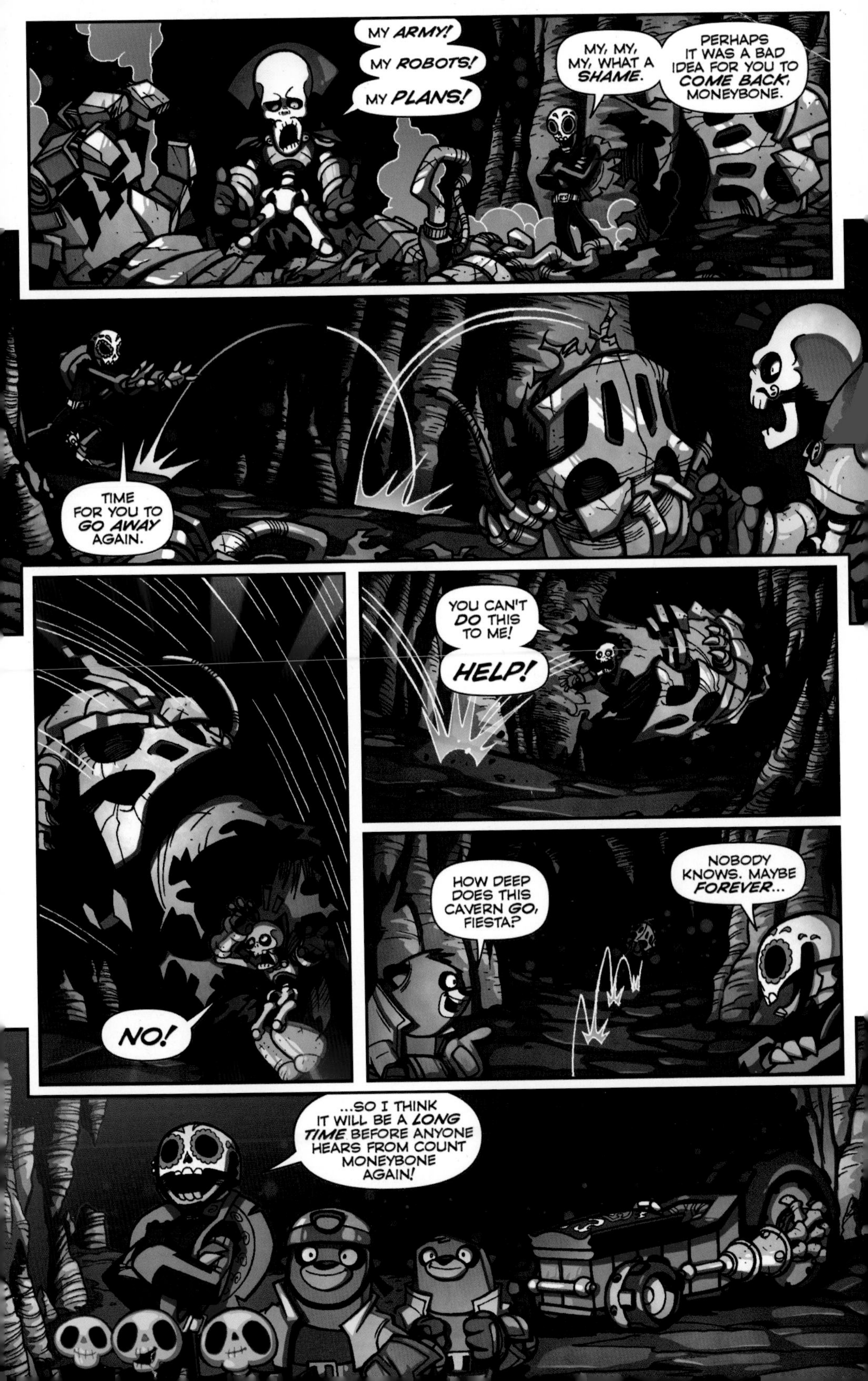
MY ARMY!
MY ROBOTS!
MY PLANS!
MY, MY, MY, WHAT A SHAME.
PERHAPS IT WAS A BAD IDEA FOR YOU TO COME BACK, MONEYBONE.
TIME FOR YOU TO GO AWAY AGAIN.
NO!
YOU CAN'T DO THIS TO ME!
HELP!
HOW DEEP DOES THIS CAVERN GO, FIESTA?
NOBODY KNOWS. MAYBE FOREVER...
...SO I THINK IT WILL BE A LONG TIME BEFORE ANYONE HEARS FROM COUNT MONEYBONE AGAIN!

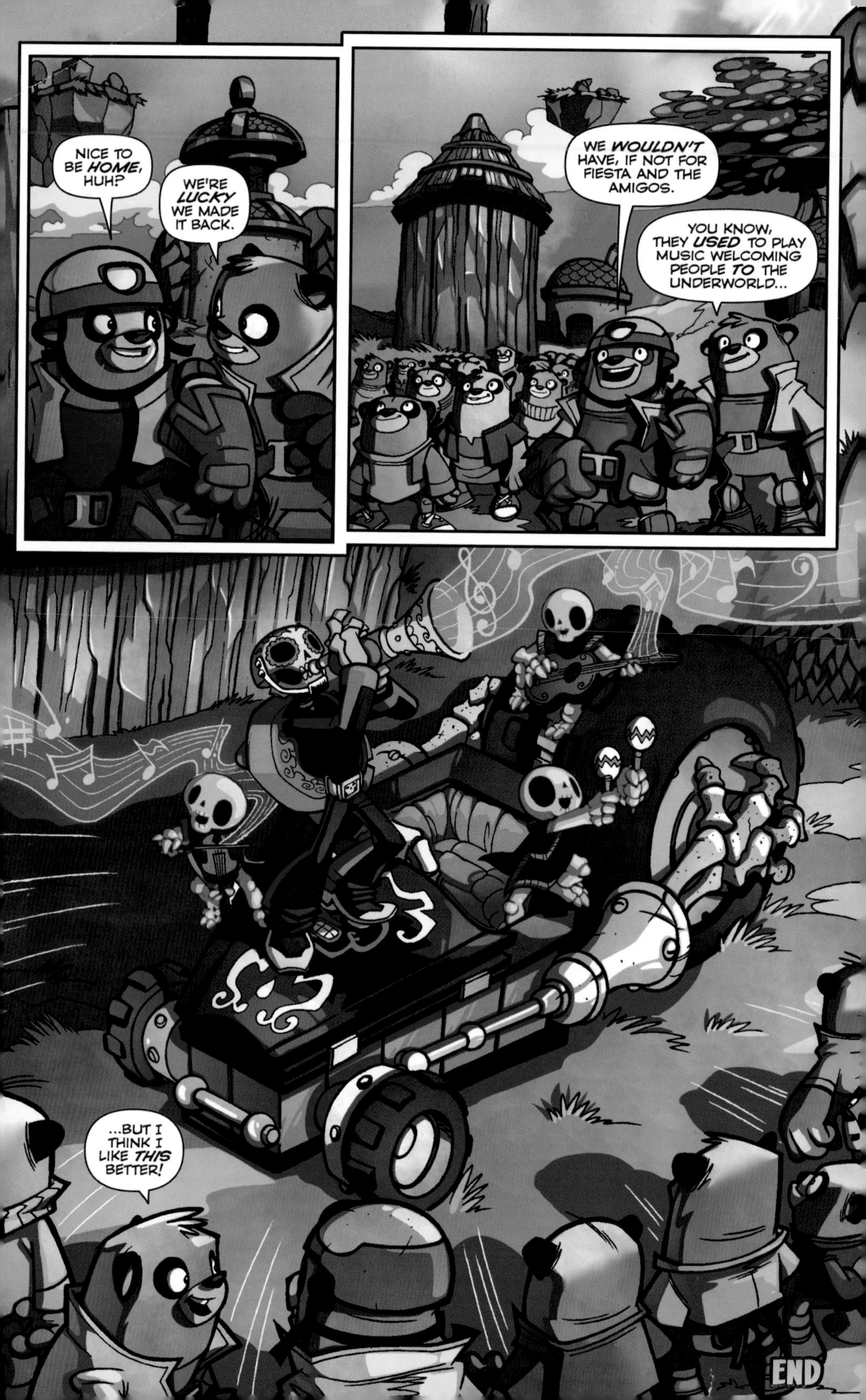
NICE TO BE HOME, HUH?
WE'RE LUCKY WE MADE IT BACK.
WE WOULDN'T HAVE, IF NOT FOR FIESTA AND THE AMIGOS.
YOU KNOW, THEY USED TO PLAY MUSIC WELCOMING PEOPLE TO THE UNDERWORLD...
...BUT I THINK I LIKE THIS BETTER!
END

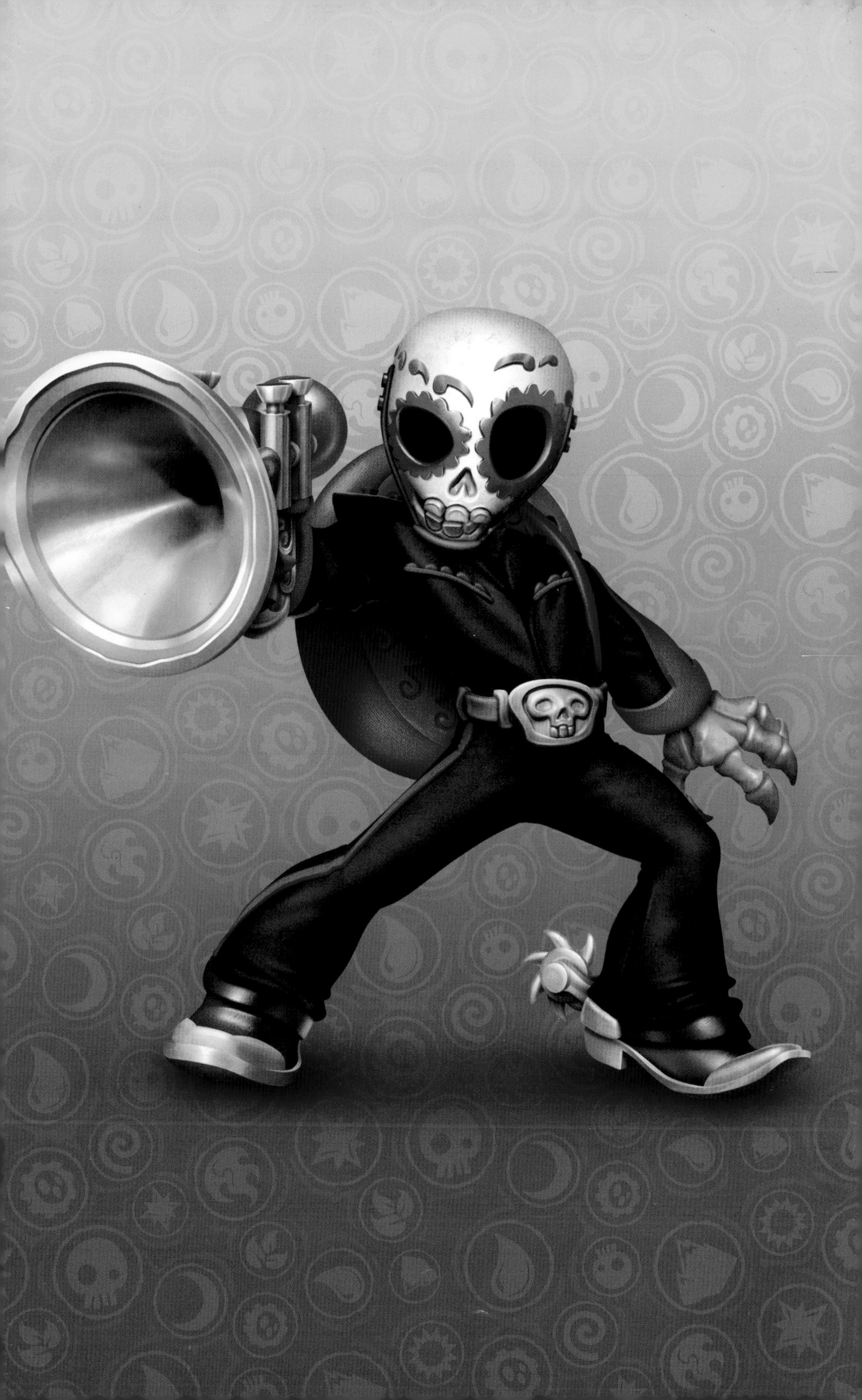

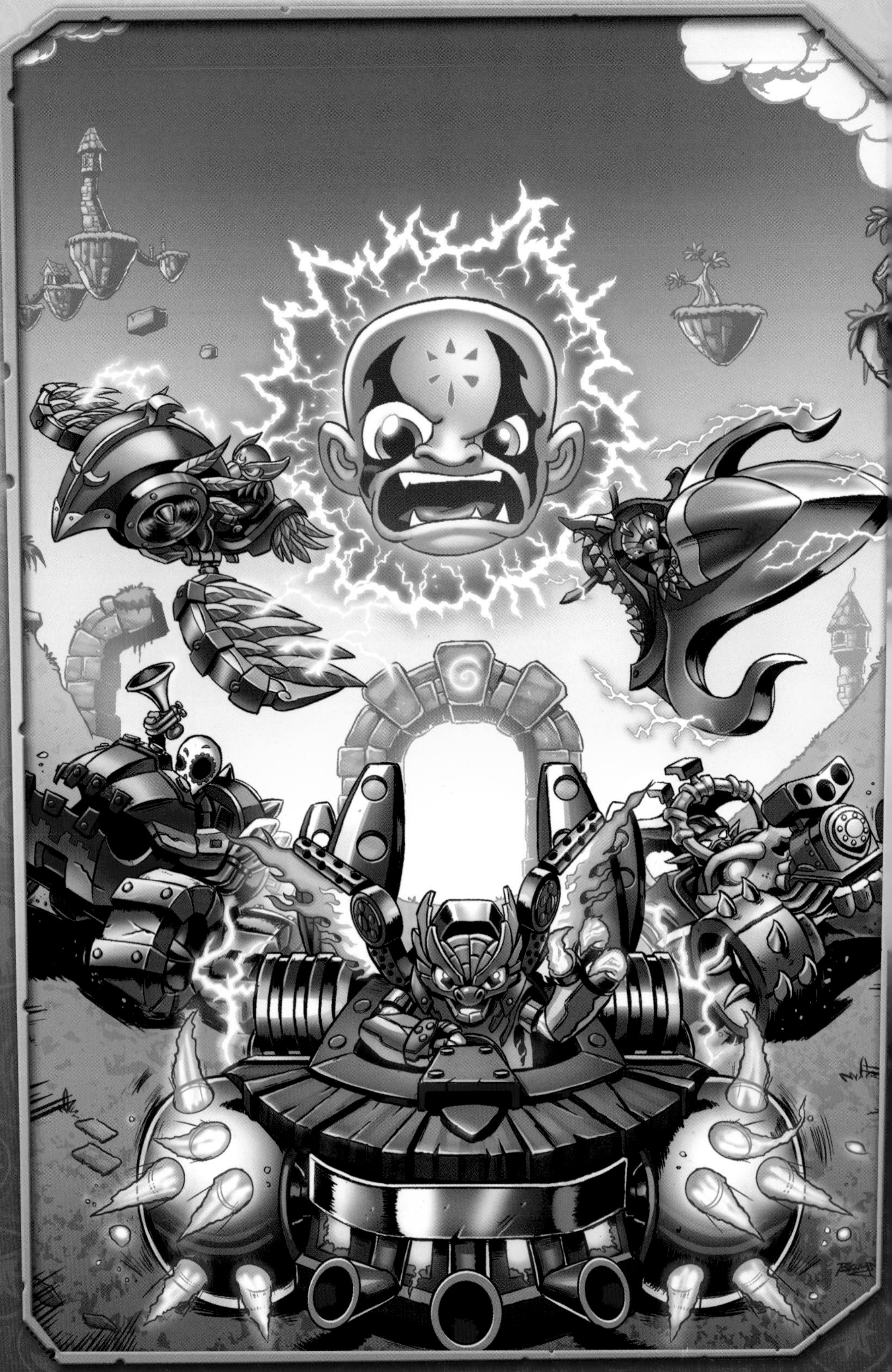

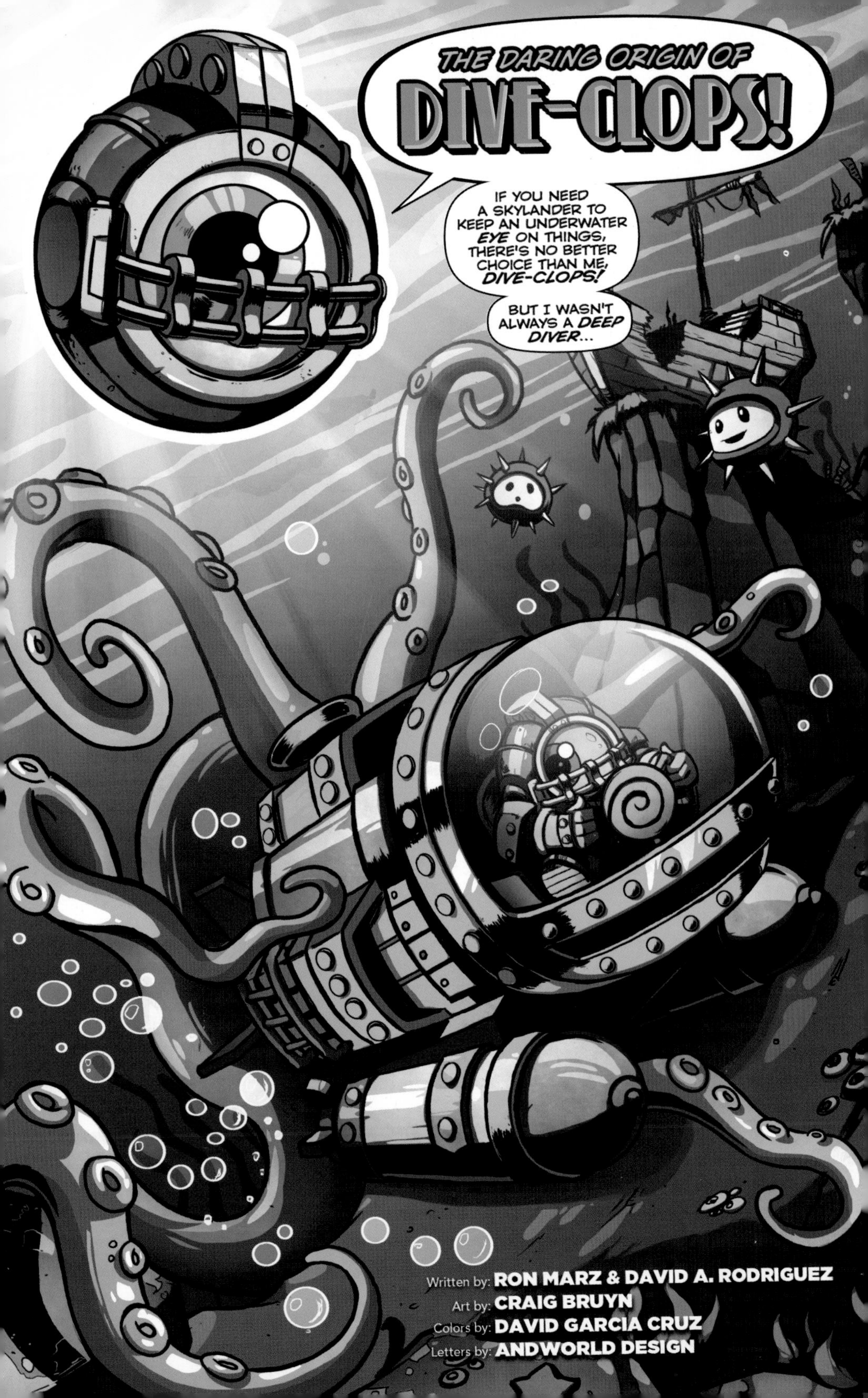
THE DARING ORIGIN OF
DIVE-CLOPS!
IF YOU NEED A SKYLANDER TO KEEP AN UNDERWATER *EYE* ON THINGS, THERE'S NO BETTER CHOICE THAN ME, *DIVE-CLOPS!*
BUT I WASN'T ALWAYS A *DEEP DIVER*...
Written by: RON MARZ & DAVID A. RODRIGUEZ
Art by: CRAIG BRUYN
Colors by: DAVID GARCIA CRUZ
Letters by: ANDWORLD DESIGN

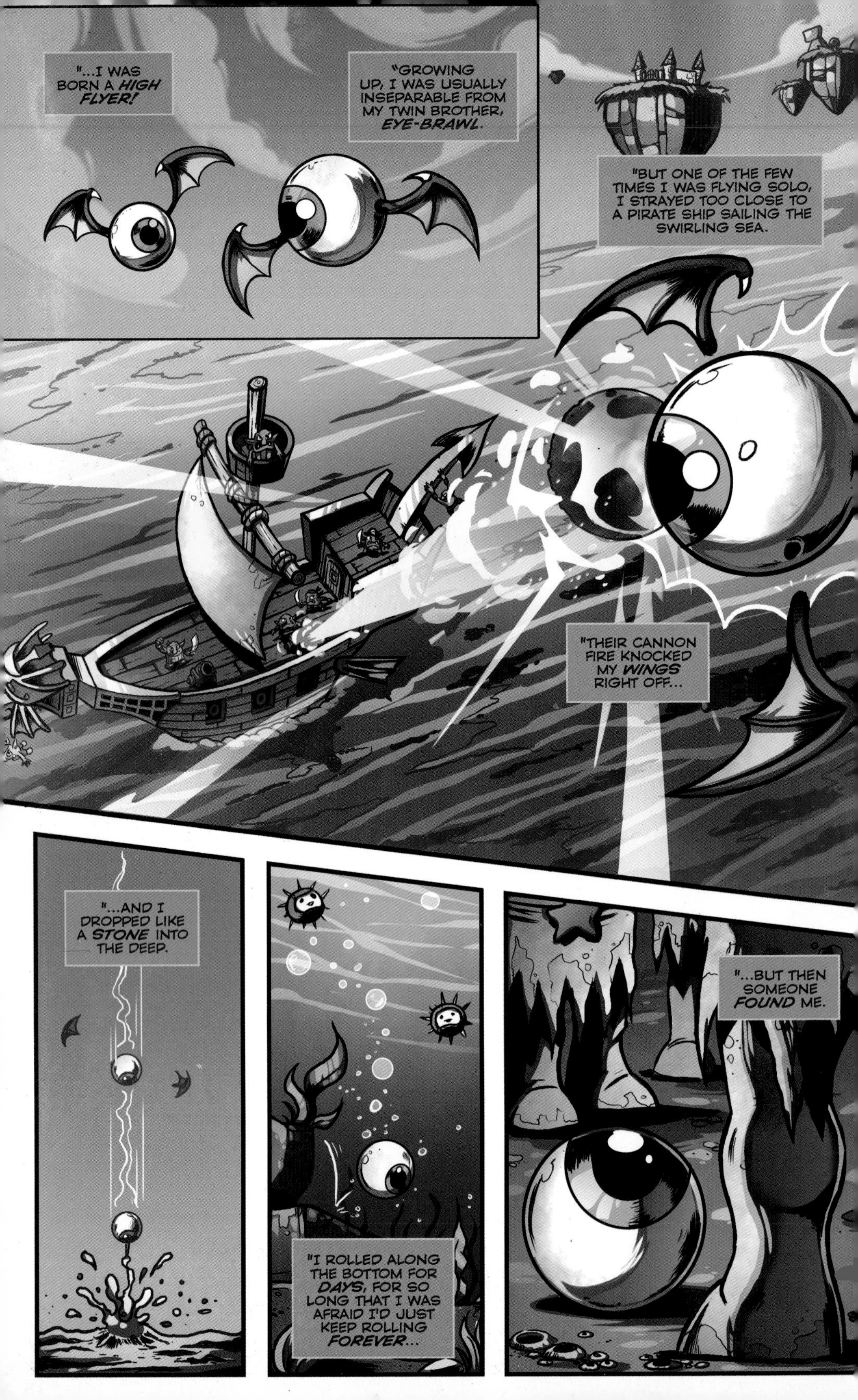
"...I WAS BORN A HIGH FLYER!
"GROWING UP, I WAS USUALLY INSEPARABLE FROM MY TWIN BROTHER, EYE-BRAWL.
"BUT ONE OF THE FEW TIMES I WAS FLYING SOLO, I STRAYED TOO CLOSE TO A PIRATE SHIP SAILING THE SWIRLING SEA.
"THEIR CANNON FIRE KNOCKED MY WINGS RIGHT OFF...
"...AND I DROPPED LIKE A STONE INTO THE DEEP.
"I ROLLED ALONG THE BOTTOM FOR DAYS, FOR SO LONG THAT I WAS AFRAID I'D JUST KEEP ROLLING FOREVER...
"...BUT THEN SOMEONE FOUND ME.

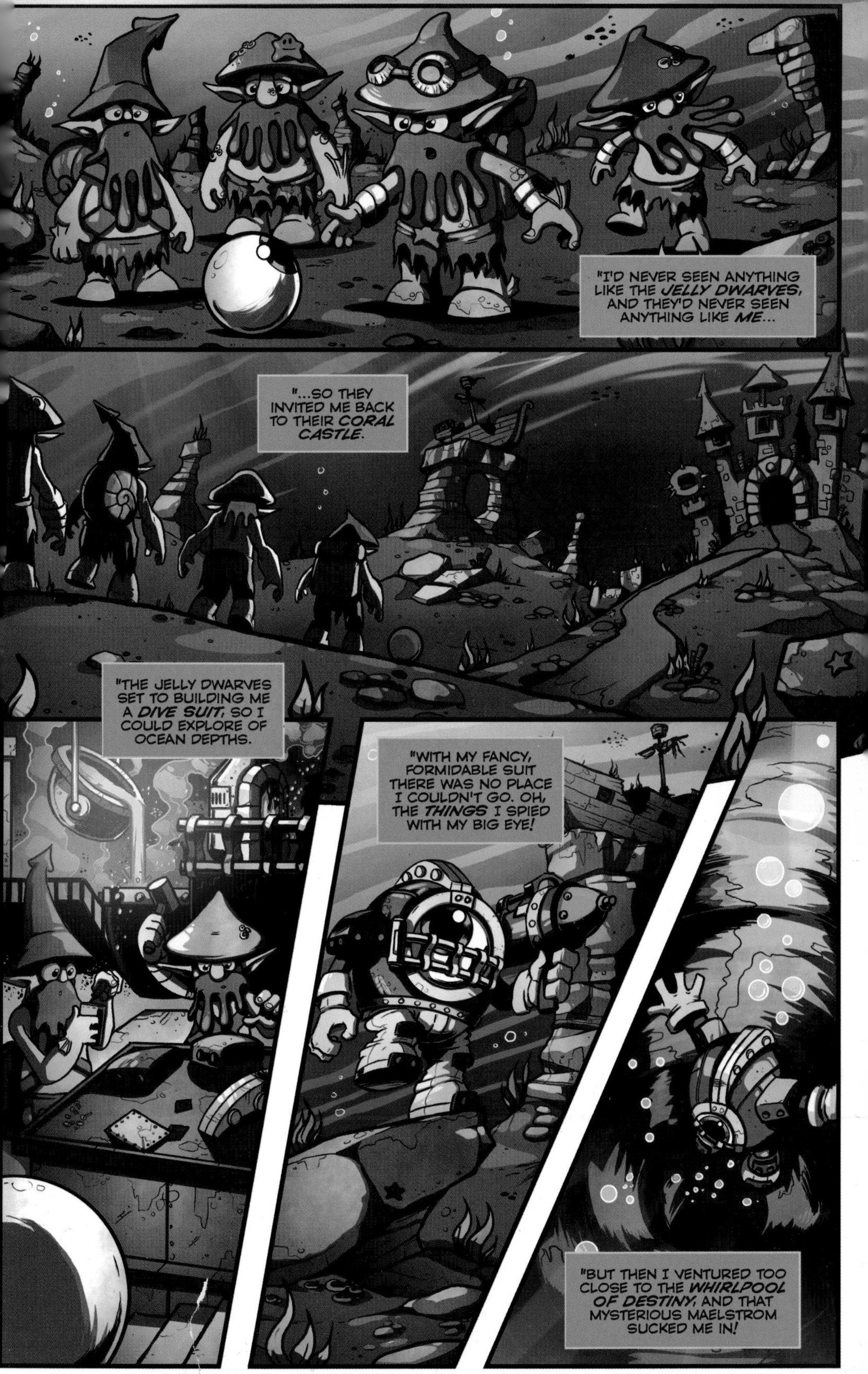
"I'D NEVER SEEN ANYTHING LIKE THE *JELLY DWARVES*, AND THEY'D NEVER SEEN ANYTHING LIKE *ME*...
"...SO THEY INVITED ME BACK TO THEIR *CORAL CASTLE*.
"THE JELLY DWARVES SET TO BUILDING ME A *DIVE SUIT*, SO I COULD EXPLORE OF OCEAN DEPTHS.
"WITH MY FANCY, FORMIDABLE SUIT THERE WAS NO PLACE I COULDN'T GO. OH, THE *THINGS* I SPIED WITH MY BIG EYE!
"BUT THEN I VENTURED TOO CLOSE TO THE *WHIRLPOOL OF DESTINY*, AND THAT MYSTERIOUS MAELSTROM SUCKED ME IN!

"I HAD NO IDEA HOW LONG I WHIRLED AND SWIRLED, BUT EVENTUALLY THE WHIRLPOOL *SPIT* ME BACK OUT..."

"...AND I DISCOVERED *THOUSANDS* OF YEARS HAS PASSED!"

"I WAS FEELING SO LOST AND ALONE, BUT *MASTER EON* APPEARED AND OFFERED ME A CHANCE TO BE A *SKYLANDER*, JUST LIKE MY BROTHER.

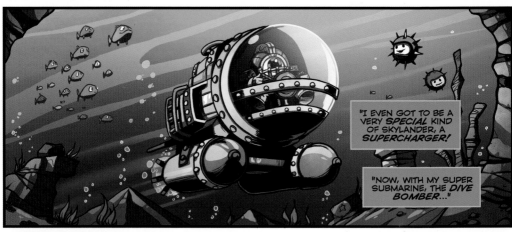

"I EVEN GOT TO BE A VERY *SPECIAL* KIND OF SKYLANDER, A *SUPERCHARGER!*

"NOW, WITH MY SUPER SUBMARINE, THE *DIVE BOMBER...*"

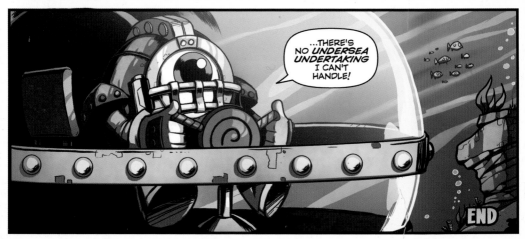

...THERE'S NO *UNDERSEA UNDERTAKING* I CAN'T HANDLE!

END

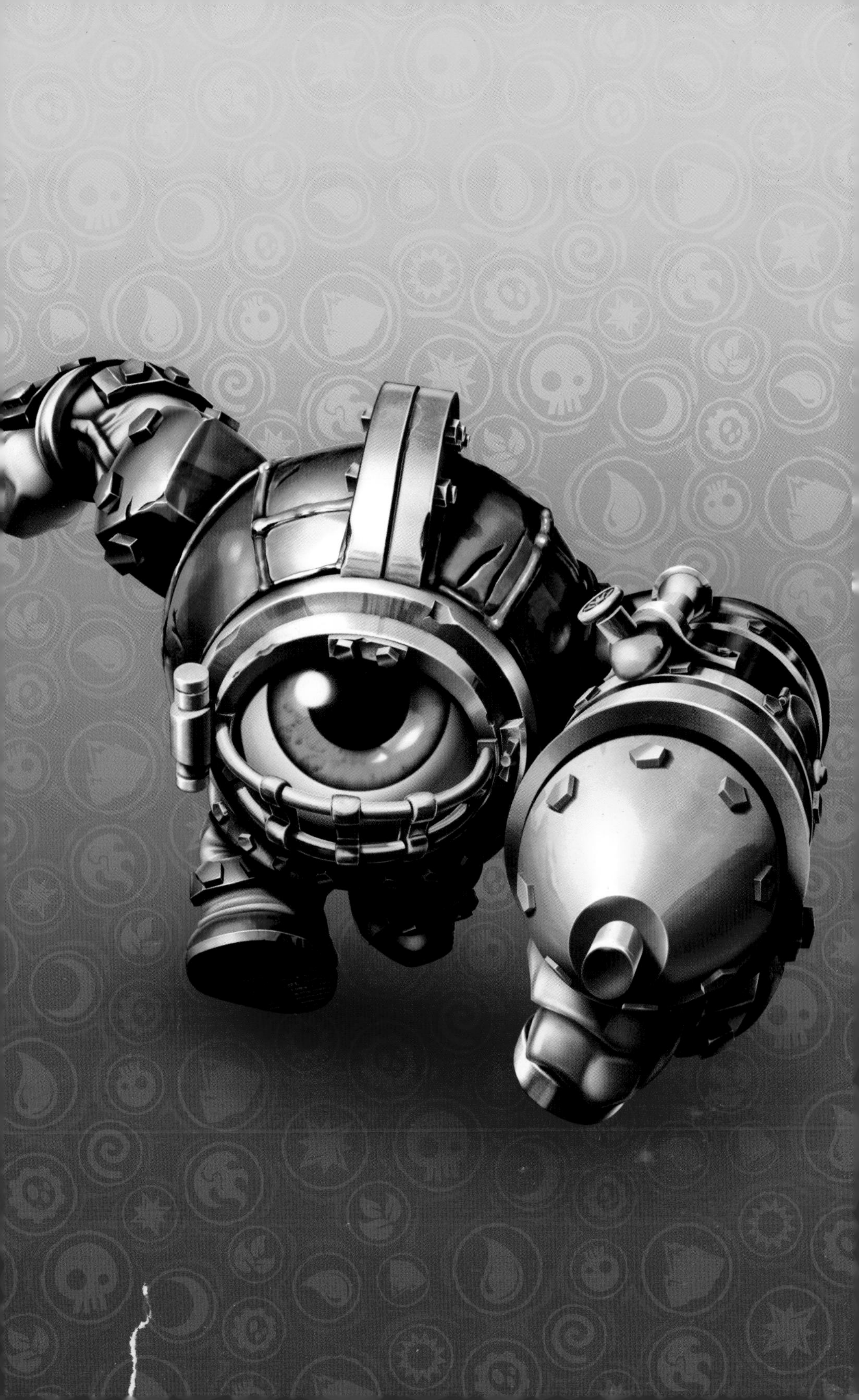

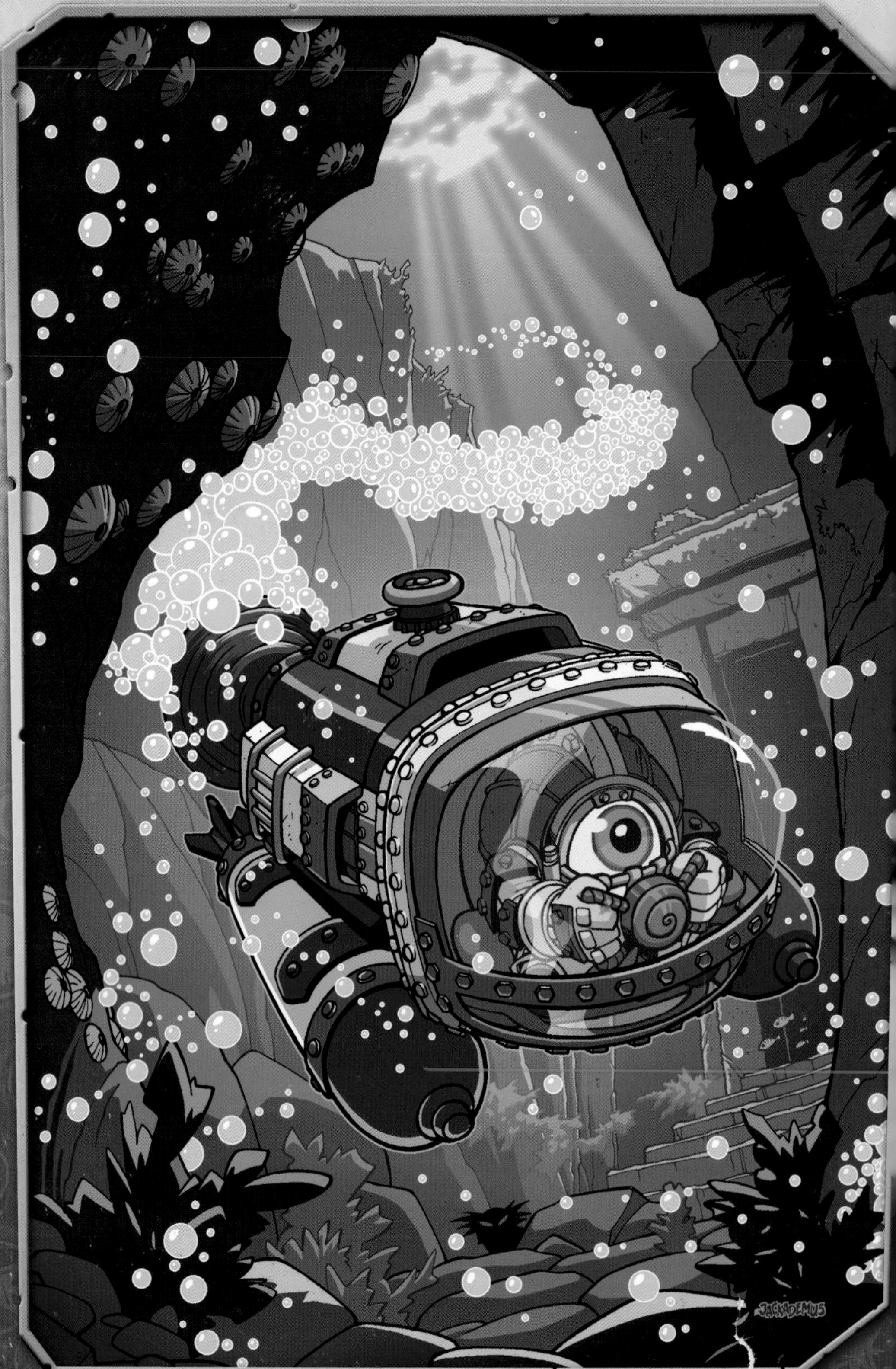
JACKADEMUS

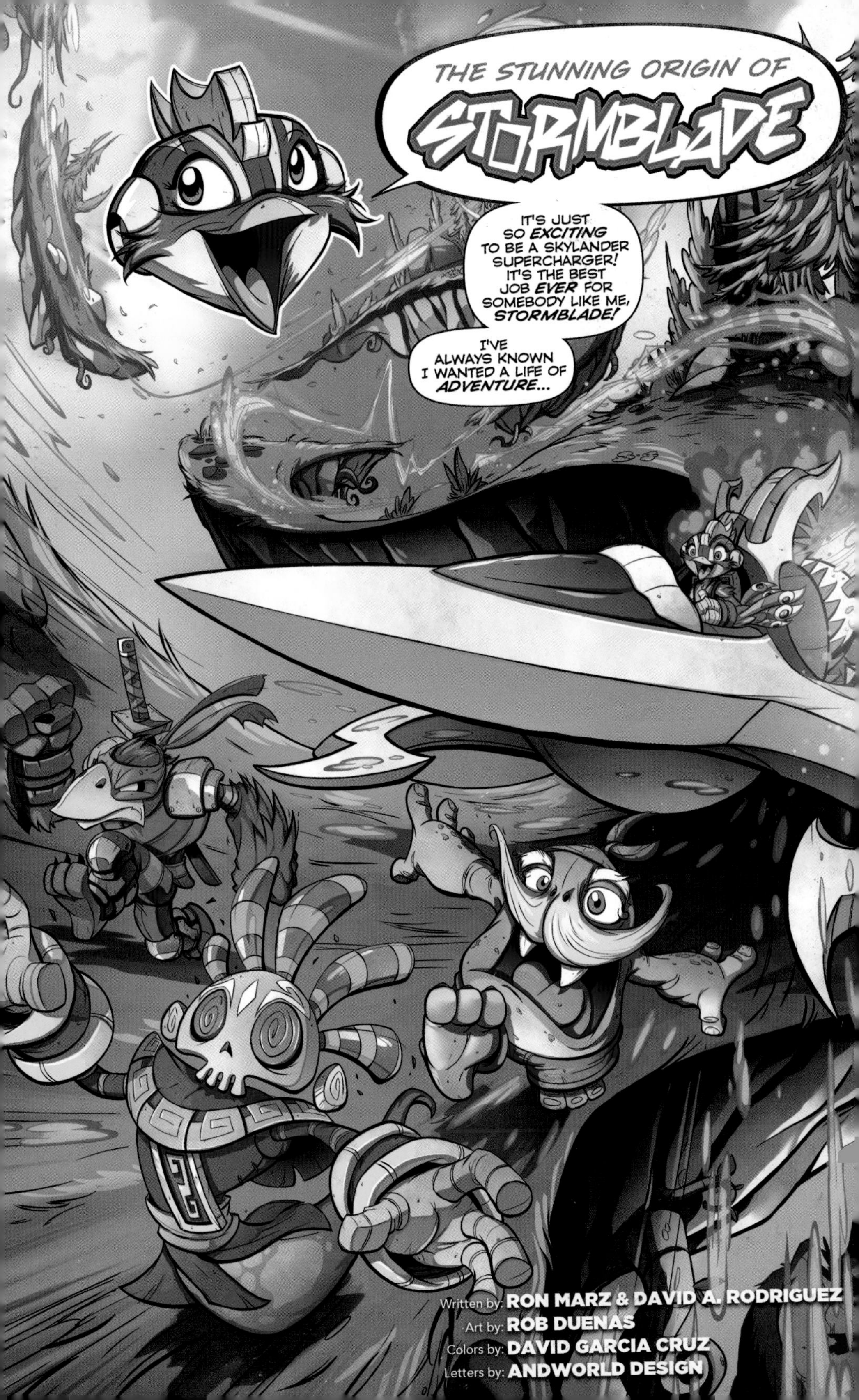
THE STUNNING ORIGIN OF
STORMBLADE
IT'S JUST SO EXCITING TO BE A SKYLANDER SUPERCHARGER! IT'S THE BEST JOB EVER FOR SOMEBODY LIKE ME, STORMBLADE!
I'VE ALWAYS KNOWN I WANTED A LIFE OF ADVENTURE...
Written by: RON MARZ & DAVID A. RODRIGUEZ
Art by: ROB DUENAS
Colors by: DAVID GARCIA CRUZ
Letters by: ANDWORLD DESIGN

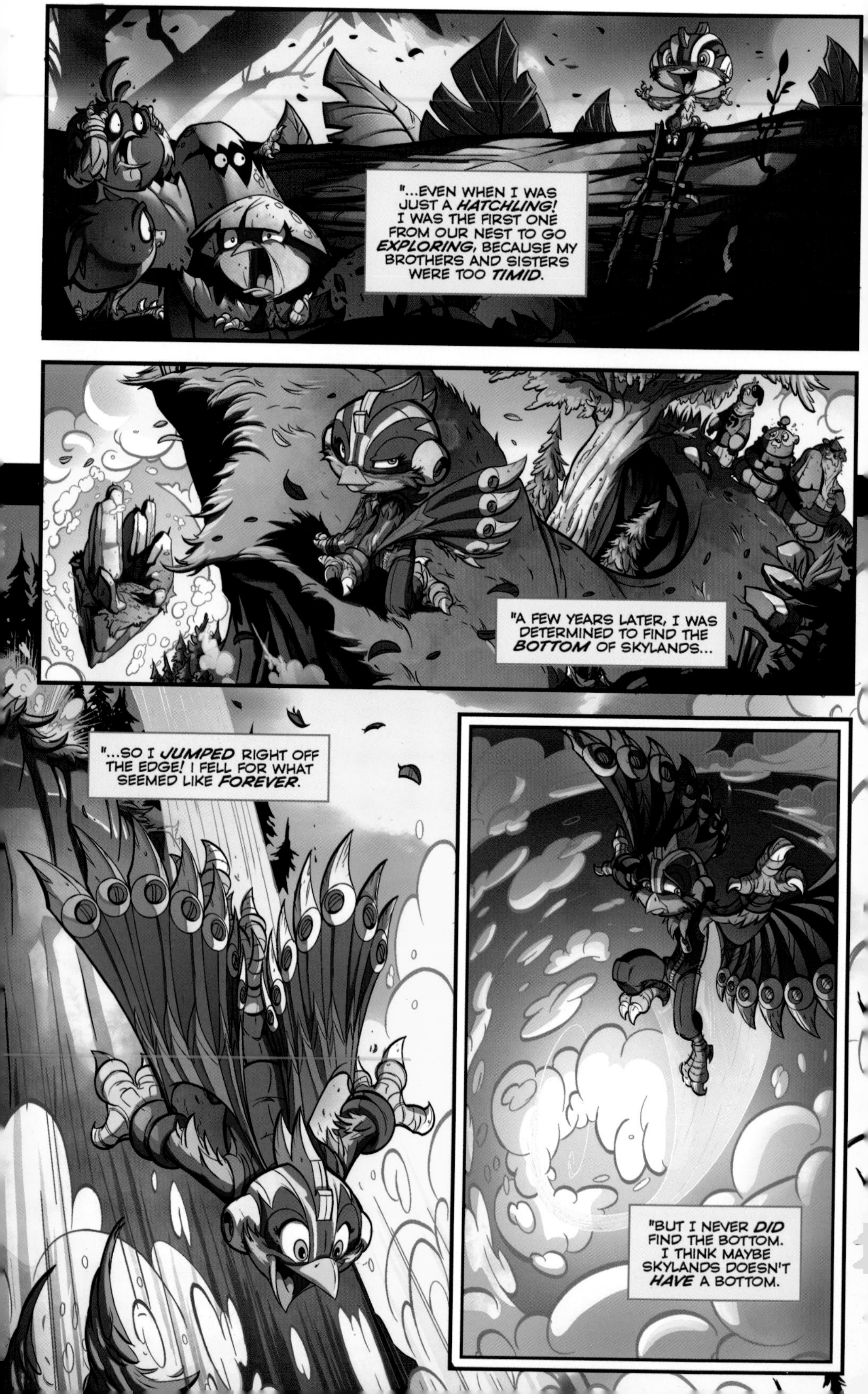
"...EVEN WHEN I WAS JUST A *HATCHLING!* I WAS THE FIRST ONE FROM OUR NEST TO GO *EXPLORING,* BECAUSE MY BROTHERS AND SISTERS WERE TOO *TIMID*.
"A FEW YEARS LATER, I WAS DETERMINED TO FIND THE *BOTTOM* OF SKYLANDS...
"...SO I *JUMPED* RIGHT OFF THE EDGE! I FELL FOR WHAT SEEMED LIKE *FOREVER*.
"BUT I NEVER *DID* FIND THE BOTTOM. I THINK MAYBE SKYLANDS DOESN'T *HAVE* A BOTTOM.

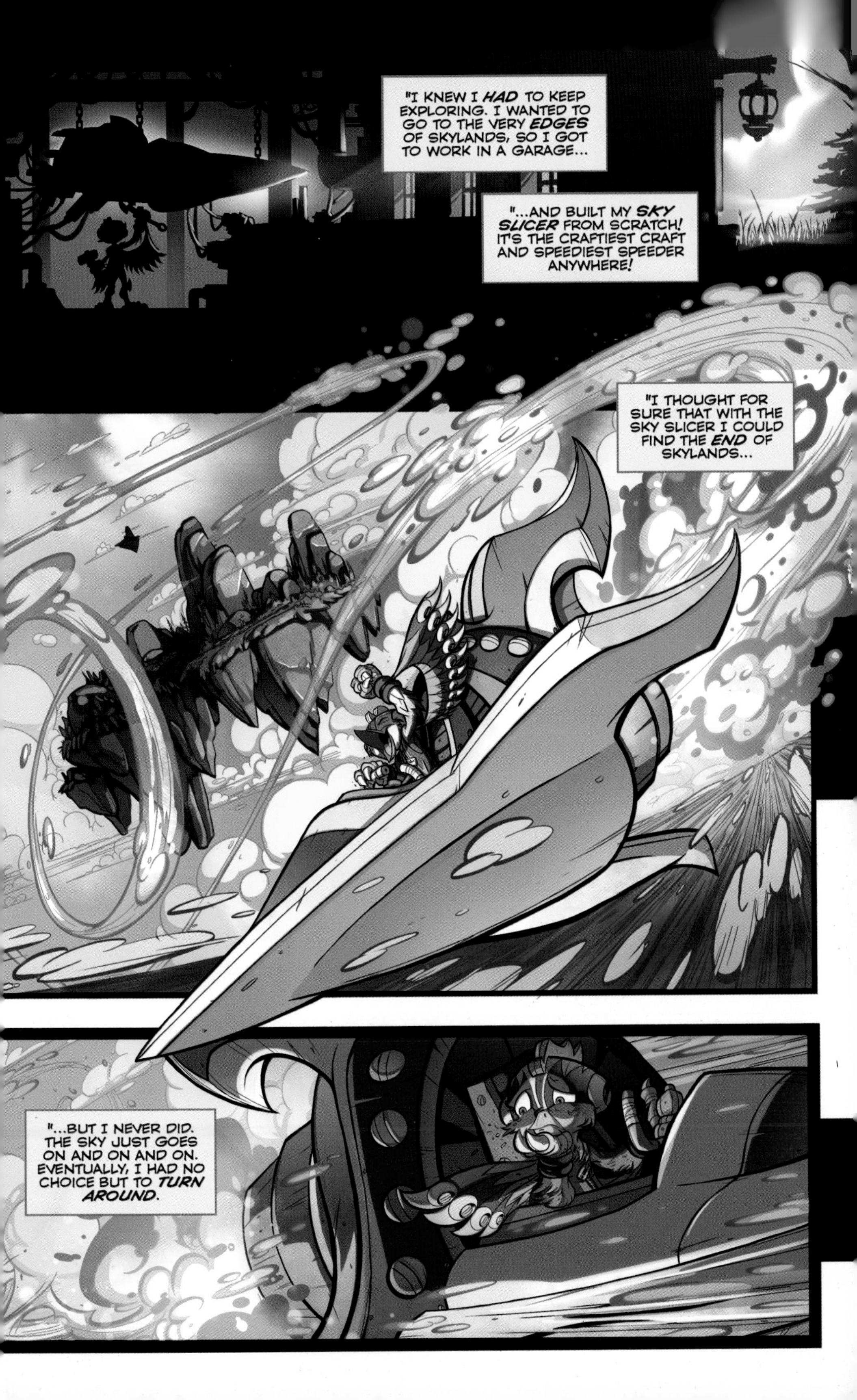
"I KNEW I HAD TO KEEP EXPLORING. I WANTED TO GO TO THE VERY EDGES OF SKYLANDS, SO I GOT TO WORK IN A GARAGE...
"...AND BUILT MY SKY SLICER FROM SCRATCH! IT'S THE CRAFTIEST CRAFT AND SPEEDIEST SPEEDER ANYWHERE!
"I THOUGHT FOR SURE THAT WITH THE SKY SLICER I COULD FIND THE END OF SKYLANDS...
"...BUT I NEVER DID. THE SKY JUST GOES ON AND ON AND ON. EVENTUALLY, I HAD NO CHOICE BUT TO TURN AROUND.

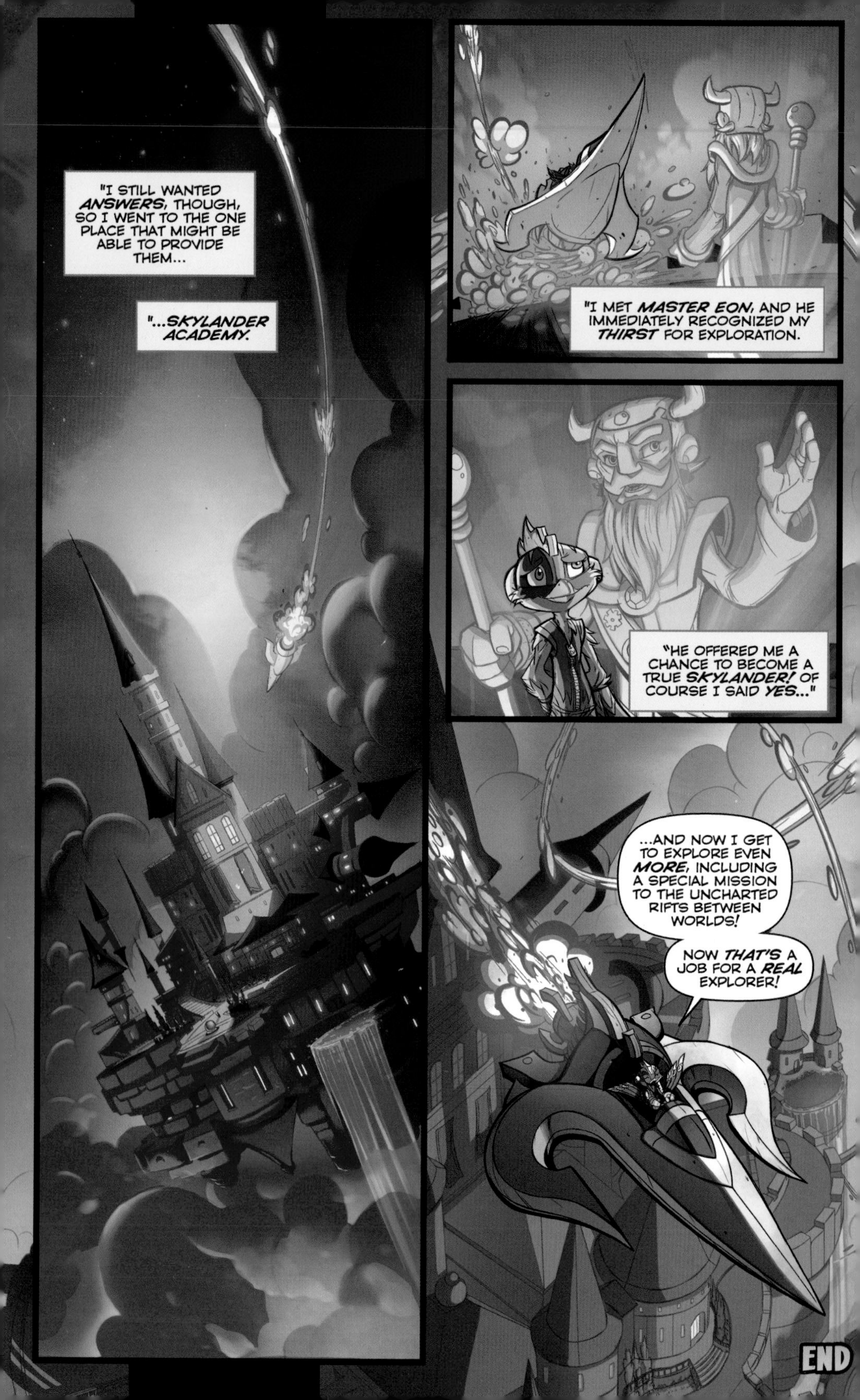
"I STILL WANTED ANSWERS, THOUGH, SO I WENT TO THE ONE PLACE THAT MIGHT BE ABLE TO PROVIDE THEM...
"...SKYLANDER ACADEMY.
"I MET MASTER EON, AND HE IMMEDIATELY RECOGNIZED MY THIRST FOR EXPLORATION.
"HE OFFERED ME A CHANCE TO BECOME A TRUE SKYLANDER! OF COURSE I SAID YES..."
...AND NOW I GET TO EXPLORE EVEN MORE, INCLUDING A SPECIAL MISSION TO THE UNCHARTED RIFTS BETWEEN WORLDS!
NOW THAT'S A JOB FOR A REAL EXPLORER!
END

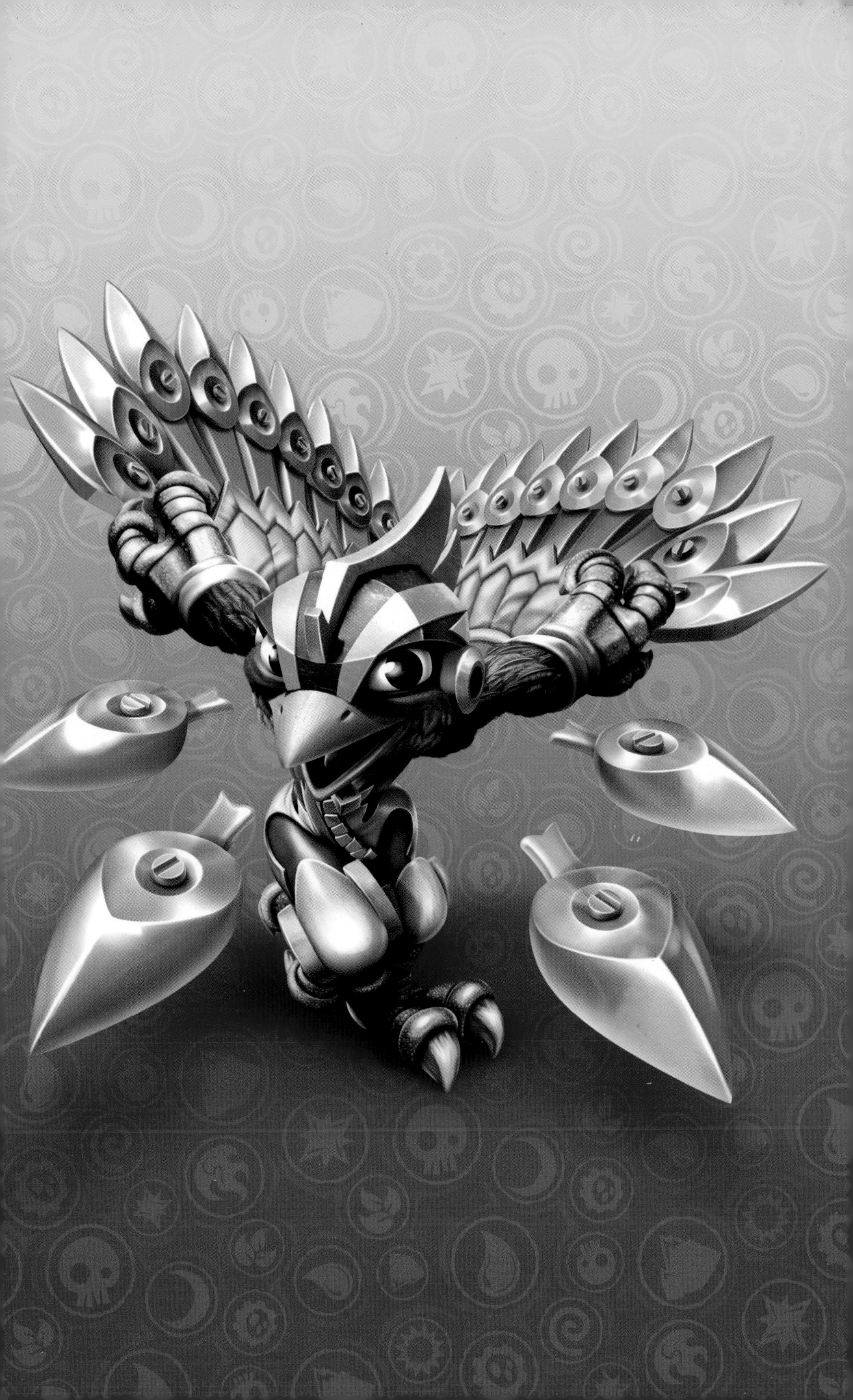

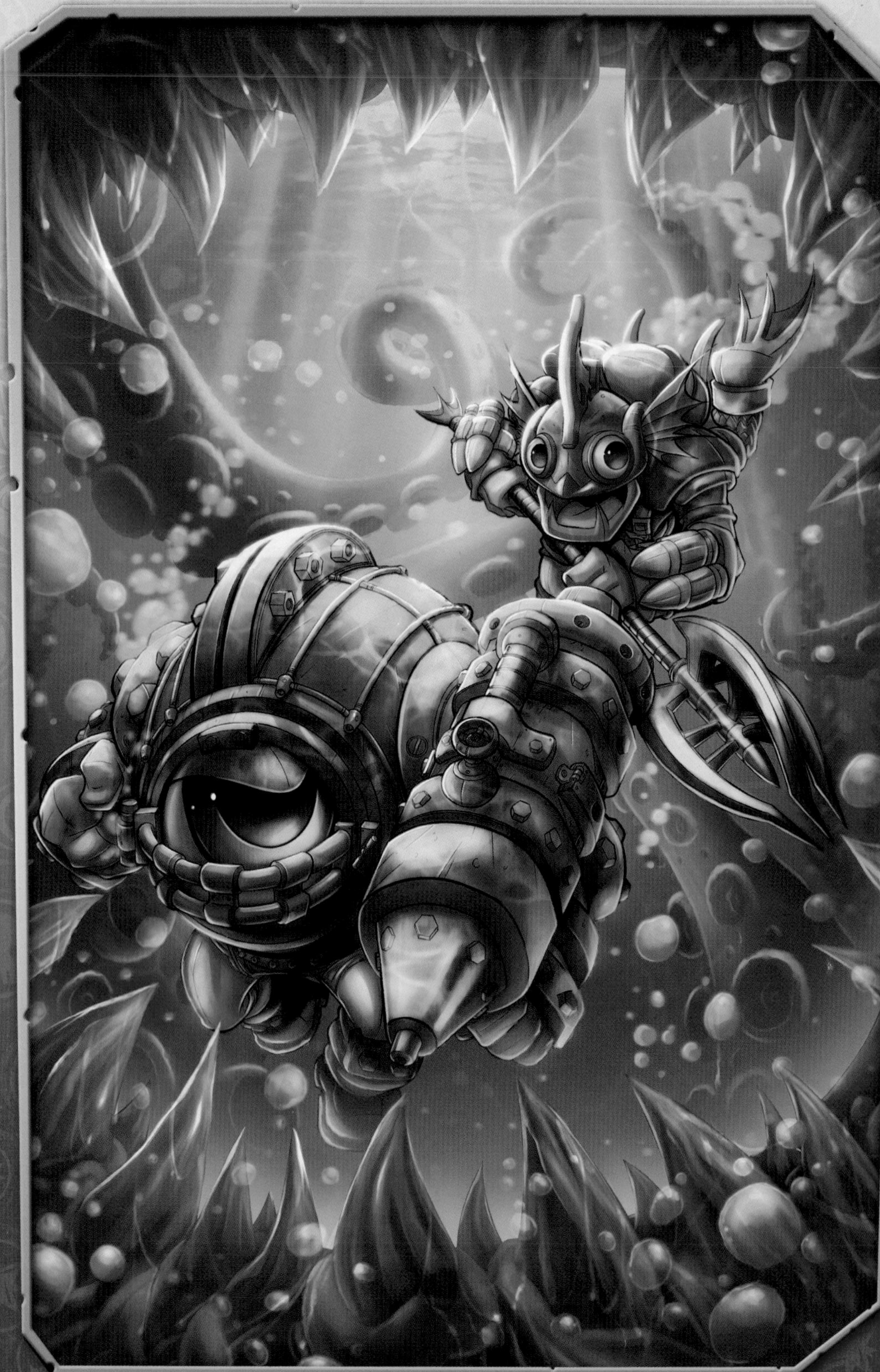

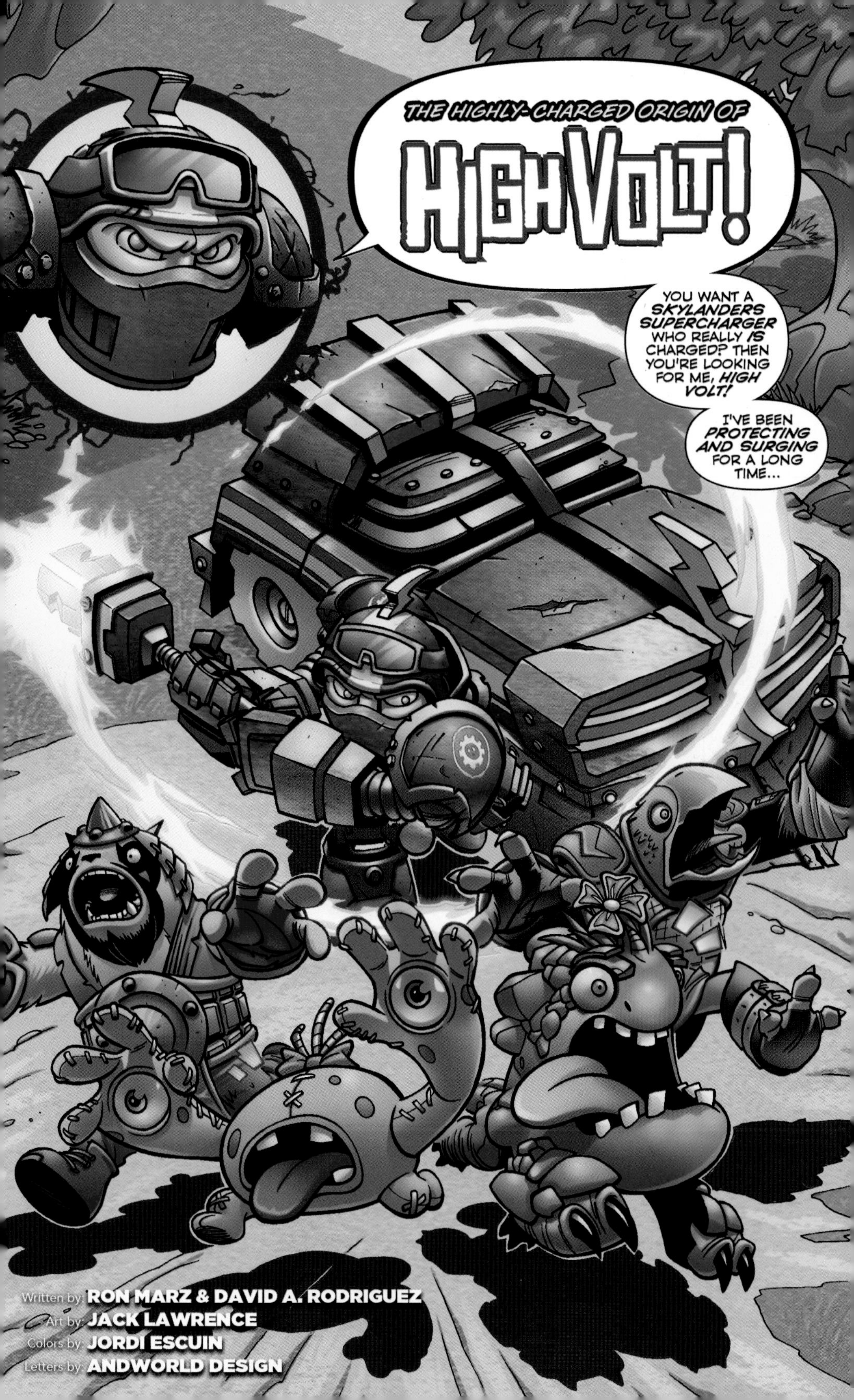
THE HIGHLY-CHARGED ORIGIN OF
HIGH VOLT!
YOU WANT A SKYLANDERS SUPERCHARGER WHO REALLY IS CHARGED? THEN YOU'RE LOOKING FOR ME, HIGH VOLT!
I'VE BEEN PROTECTING AND SURGING FOR A LONG TIME...
Written by: RON MARZ & DAVID A. RODRIGUEZ
Art by: JACK LAWRENCE
Colors by: JORDI ESCUIN
Letters by: ANDWORLD DESIGN

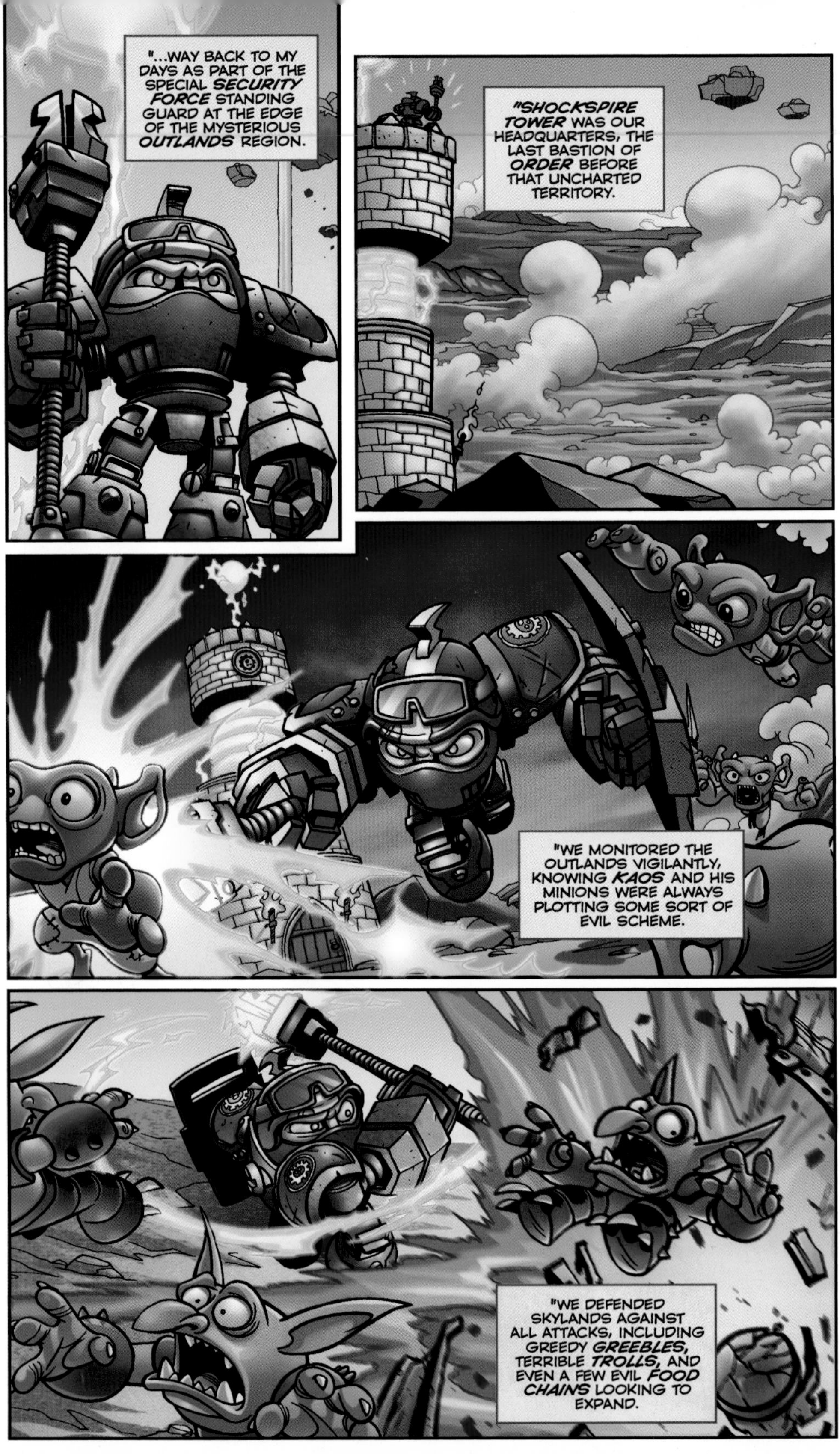
"...WAY BACK TO MY DAYS AS PART OF THE SPECIAL SECURITY FORCE STANDING GUARD AT THE EDGE OF THE MYSTERIOUS OUTLANDS REGION.
"SHOCKSPIRE TOWER WAS OUR HEADQUARTERS, THE LAST BASTION OF ORDER BEFORE THAT UNCHARTED TERRITORY.
"WE MONITORED THE OUTLANDS VIGILANTLY, KNOWING KAOS AND HIS MINIONS WERE ALWAYS PLOTTING SOME SORT OF EVIL SCHEME.
"WE DEFENDED SKYLANDS AGAINST ALL ATTACKS, INCLUDING GREEDY GREEBLES, TERRIBLE TROLLS, AND EVEN A FEW EVIL FOOD CHAINS LOOKING TO EXPAND.

"ON ONE PATROL, I DROVE MY SPECIALLY BUILT *SHIELD STRIKER* DEEPER INTO THE OUTLANDS THAN I'D EVER BEEN...

"...AND I WAS *STUNNED* AT WHAT I FOUND.

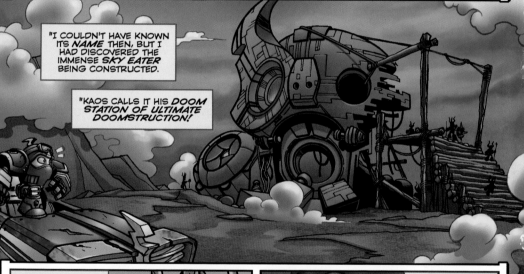

"I COULDN'T HAVE KNOWN ITS *NAME* THEN, BUT I HAD DISCOVERED THE IMMENSE *SKY EATER* BEING CONSTRUCTED.

"KAOS CALLS IT HIS *DOOM STATION OF ULTIMATE DOOMSTRUCTION!*

"HIS *CYCLOPS TROOPS* TRIED TO OVERWHELM ME...

"...BUT I WAS ABLE TO *ESCAPE* BY THE SLIMMEST OF MARGINS.

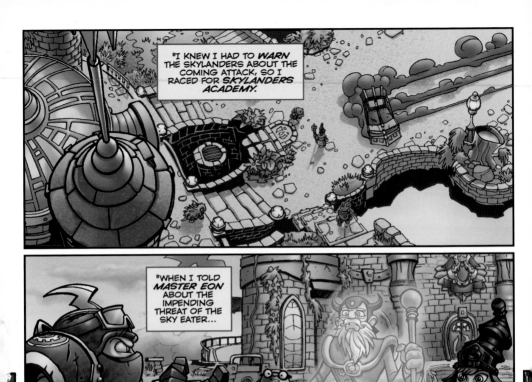

"I KNEW I HAD TO *WARN* THE SKYLANDERS ABOUT THE COMING ATTACK, SO I RACED FOR *SKYLANDERS ACADEMY.*

"WHEN I TOLD *MASTER EON* ABOUT THE IMPENDING THREAT OF THE SKY EATER...

"...HE ASKED ME TO BECOME AN *OFFICIAL* SKYLANDER, AND BATTLE ALONGSIDE THE GREATEST HEROES EVER.

"OBVIOUSLY I *ACCEPTED* ON THE SPOT...

...AND NOW I CAN PROMISE YOU, EVILDOERS ARE DEFINITELY IN FOR A *SHOCK!*

END

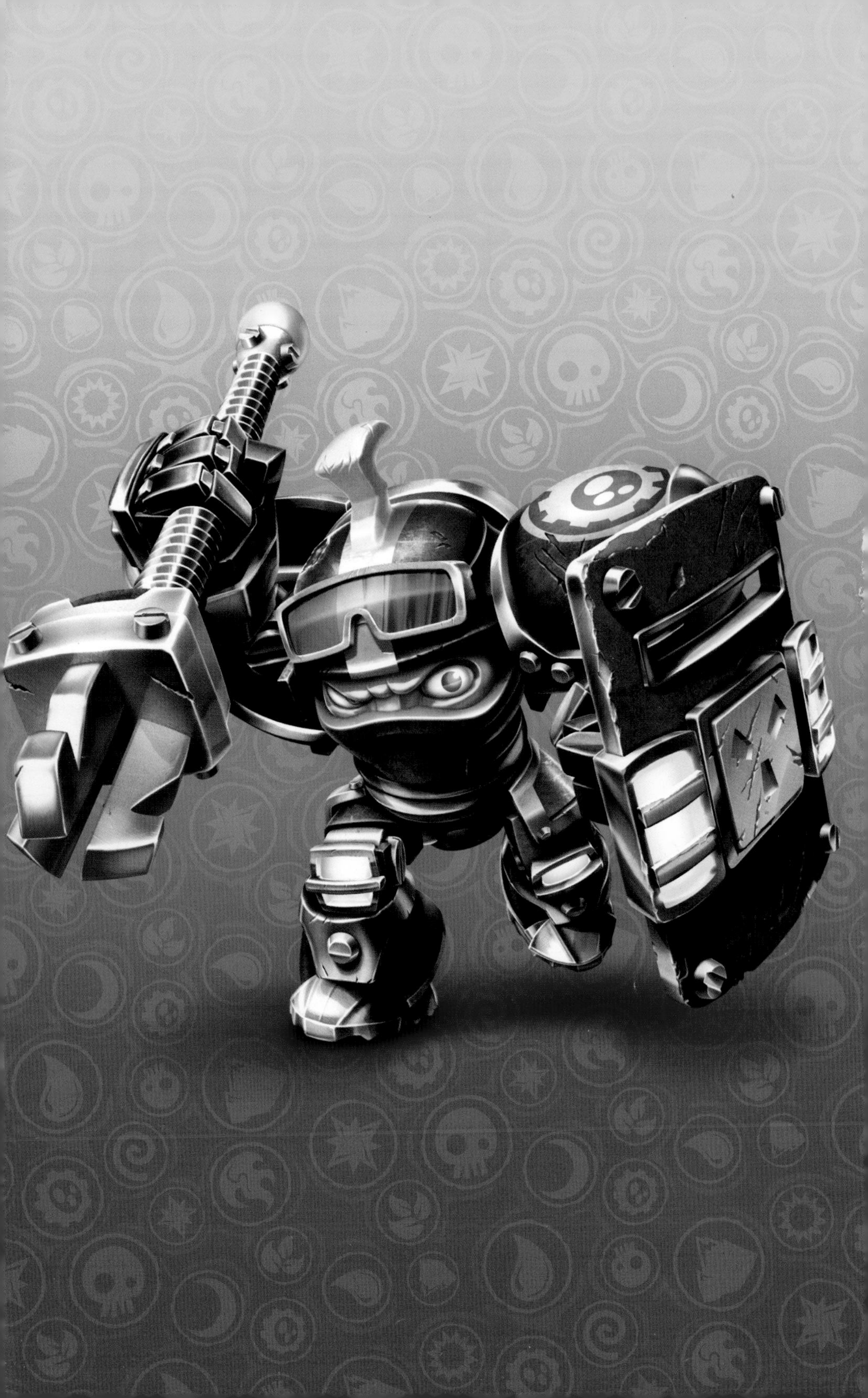

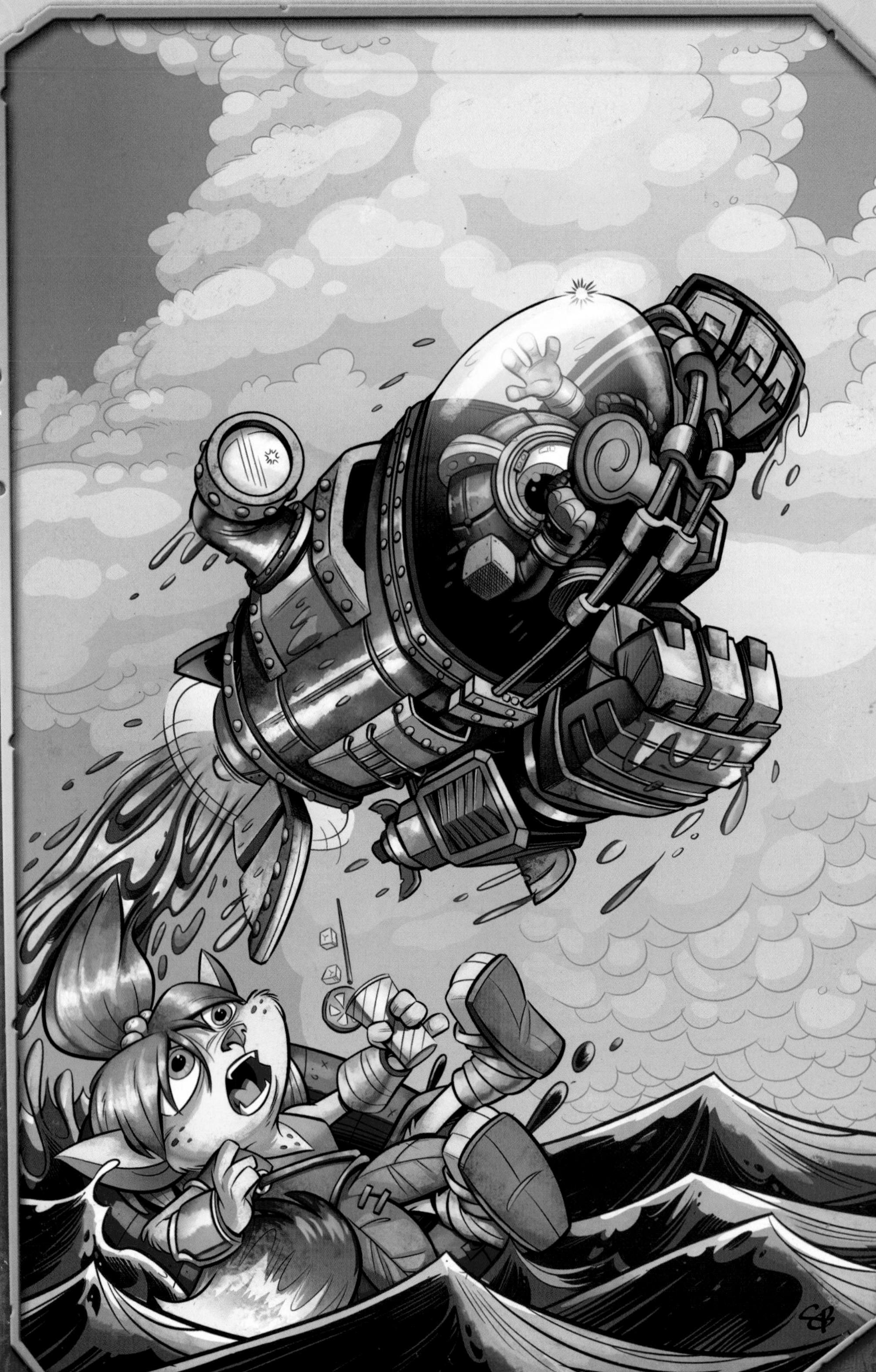

SKYLANDERS SUPERCHARGERS

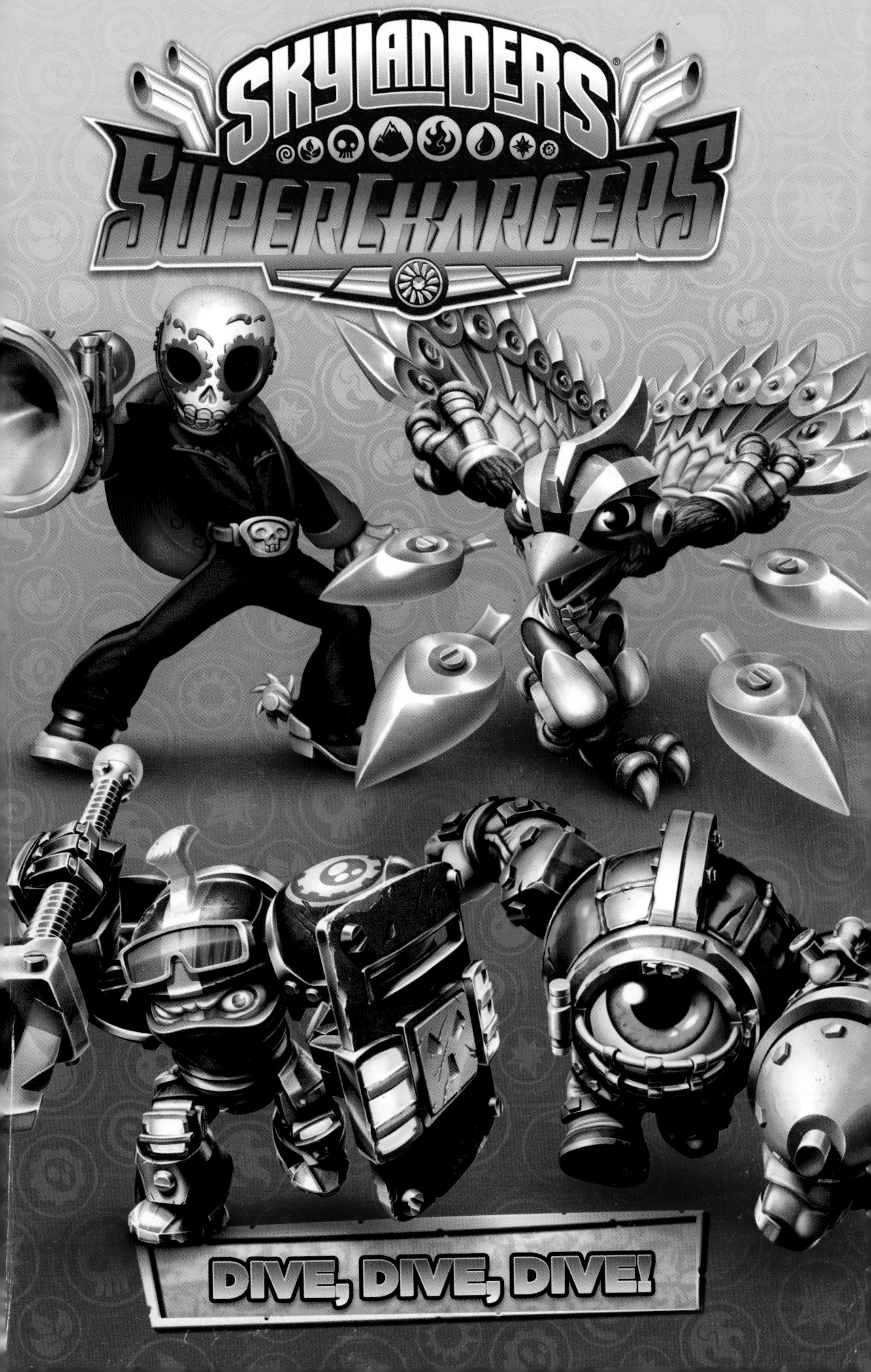

DIVE, DIVE, DIVE!

SKYLANDERS

SKYLANDERS™ THE KAOS TRAP
ISBN: 978-1-63140-141-1

SKYLANDERS™ RETURN OF THE DRAGON KING
ISBN: 978-1-63140-268-5

SKYLANDERS™ CHAMPIONS
ISBN: 978-1-63140-229-6

SKYLANDERS™ RIFT INTO OVERDRIVE
ISBN: 978-1-63140-581-5

SKYLANDERS™ SECRET AGENT SECRETS
ISBN: 978-1-63140-412-2

FIND MORE SKYLANDERS™ COMICS

COMIC SHOP LOCATOR SERVICE
888-COMIC-BOOK
comicshoplocator.com

IDW®